The Soul

The Legend of the Future

The Soul

The Legend of the Future

by Luiza Dobrzynska

PAPERBACK ISBN: 978-1-7348606-6-5

EPUB ISBN: 978-1-3936345-7-7

***

WRITTEN BY LUIZA DOBRZYNSKA

PUBLISHED BY ROYAL HAWAIIAN PRESS

COVER ART BY TYRONE ROSHANTHA

TRANSLATED BY MONIKA WIKLIK

PUBLISHING ASSISTANCE: BALASUBRAMANIAN NAMBI

***

FOR MORE WORKS BY THIS AUTHOR, PLEASE VISIT:

WWW.ROYALHAWAIIANPRESS.COM

***

VERSION NUMBER 1.00

Motto:

Soul is the essence of existence,
The life shining in tired eyes,
Which, in search of solace,
Look for the moon at night.
The soul is an intangible self,
In its being indescribable,
But believe it, it is all too real,
When one is seeking solace
From everyday life

Weronika Bąk

Introduction

The school was large, all glazed tile, sterile clean, guarded by an electronic system and trained security personnel. The safety of the young generation was a priority. From the moment two people received permission to have a child, everything was subject to the strict control imposed by the Department of Genetic Selection. The child admitted to the child-rearing process had to meet certain conditions—primarily to be physically and mentally healthy, and promising to develop an IQ in accordance with applicable standards. Otherwise the child was euthanized without asking their parents' permission. They had no say in that. If they wanted to be parents at all, they had to accept all the restrictions and legal orders. They could not neglect visits to the pediatrician or child psychologist, or isolate their offspring from peers. The child had to develop harmoniously in order to become a useful member of society.

Not everyone was able to enjoy the prospect of bringing children into the world and raising future citizens. A twenty-four-year-old graduate of the history department at the University of Sao Paulo, Estrella Federica Solis, wasn't ever going to become a mother. Her genetic qualifications, assessed right after birth, excluded that possibility. But Estrella loved children and therefore rejected an offer to work at the Central Institute of South American Archeology for the position of an elementary school teacher in one of the primary schools. It wasn't an inferior position—the upbringing of children under the age of ten was treated very seriously and only highly qualified professionals with impeccable curricula were allowed to work with them. And Etta was just that...

I

And why was it so bad in those times?" asked a chubby little girl with pigtails from the second row.

"Because, Jodie, people did not follow sense then, but rather their feelings," the teacher answered. "They thought it was right, but it was faulty reasoning. Many children were born with a variety of defects that made them a burden to society for the rest of their lives. It took centuries to change the way of thinking of entire societies, and for some time even a kind of terror was necessary. Although today the thought of the cruelty of that time is frightening to us, it was necessary to finally come up with a model of a planetary community in which the next generation is planned sensibly, not only with love but also with logic."

The teacher had dark blonde hair, arranged in neatly curled locks, a delicate teenager's face with an insecure smile on small lips, and gray eyes with a black border around the iris. Although she was healthy and strong, she looked as fragile as a butterfly. Her name was Estrella Solis, but everyone, including the children, called her Etta.

"Miss Etta, what if someone had a baby without permission?" Waylon blurted out, a freckled redhead sitting in a seat by the window, seven years old and lively like a spark, the youngest in her group.

"It is unlikely today." Etta smiled apologetically. "We are civilized, after all. However, the penal code still covers such offenses and treats them as a crime against humanity."

"Why?"

"Just think about it, Waylon, and you'll understand. Only people who are genetically healthy are allowed to have children, because it guarantees a high probability of birthing a healthy and strong baby, and all children should be like that. Before, by allowing themselves to give birth to a sick child, its parents committed a crime against the child, who suffered for the rest of its life, and against the society that had to support it. It was not understood then, but now it is clear to everyone and nothing would justify such an act."

"But if a baby without a leg is born anyway? Or without hands?" insisted Waylon, not wanting to let go of the thread of questioning.

Etta felt her lips go dry and pale. She had to answer, but for a moment her voice refused to obey her.

"It doesn't happen," she said finally. "Such children are not born. It is not allowed. If, however... then such a miserable creature is immediately put to sleep."

"Gets a blow to the head," said the gloomily fair-haired Esteban, whose mother, after getting poisoned in the laboratory by mercury vapors, had miscarried two crippled babies and received a life-long ban on further reproduction, although her genetic fitness was high. The eight-year-old boy, plump, ruddy, full of energy and quick to laugh, became a completely different child after this misfortune. He started to make gloomy remarks, didn't play with other children, and liked reading adult horror books, stealing them skillfully from bookstores or straight from the web. His mother couldn't discourage him from this harmful hobby.

Several girls went pale, and one began to sob.

"It's not true," protested Etta. "Paulina, stop crying. Sonia, Kari, wipe your eyes. Esteban unnecessarily exaggerates; no one hits such children on their heads. They are put to sleep painlessly and quickly. This is better for everyone. Also for you, because you don't have to take care them, and someone would have to, after all."

"And do you have children?" someone from the last row shouted.

Etta shook her head. "No, honey," she said. "My genes are defective, excluding the possibility of obtaining a childbearing license."

"And you are not husbanded?" Jodie squealed timidly. She had a funny inclination to make up words and phrases, sometimes so ridiculous that Etta struggled to stay serious.

"We say 'married'," the teacher corrected her. "No, I am not. Few men would like to marry a 'zero' woman. But never mind me, dear kids. Who can remind us the degrees of procreation fitness?"

"Me!" Keen, the best student in class, exclaimed and stood up, full of self-importance. "Zero, more than twenty-five percent chance of uncertain genes. One, less than twenty-five, but more than twenty percent. Two, less than twenty percent, but more than fifteen. Three, less than fifteen percent, but more than eight. Acceptable statistical deviations are indicated by 'plus' or 'minus' signs."

"And?"

"And 'unlimited', less than eight percent chance of uncertain genes."

"Perfect, Keen. What do these numbers mean?"

"A permitted number of pregnancies."

"Not children?" Etta asked a tricky question.

"No, ma'am. Because more than one baby can be born, right?"

He smiled with satisfaction and sat down. Etta looked affectionately at her group of toddlers. As a history teacher and an educator at a primary school, she dealt exclusively with children under the age of ten, often lively and frisky, but much nicer than teens. She liked to work with them, although in truth, with her education, she would easily find a job at a serious research institute.

"It is kinda sad to be alone," Linda said softly, a serious girl with caramel-colored skin and a bunch of stiff braids around her shapely head.

"I'm not alone." The teacher smiled at her. "I have Raul."

The classroom became noisy, the children twittering like birds. Artificial people awoke the imagination of the young generation, who saw them as large dolls with which they could play house or tag.

"You have an android?"

"What is he like?"

"Is it true that they are like people?"

"Does he think?"

"What does he eat?"

"One moment, kids, wait a minute, not everybody at once. The topic of today's lesson does not cover androids... Although, we have gone quite far along the schedule, and you are a very well behaved and diligent class, so if you want we can have a short break for a chat."

"Yes, we do! Please!"

"So, can anybody tell me what you know about androids?"

A girl from the second row, Tracy Schotz, raised her hand, stood up, and recited in a single breath, "An android is a man-made, independent-thinking creature. All androids have names beginning with the letter R, from the word 'robot', according to the idea of a medieval writer, Isaac Asimov. The word 'robot' is, in turn, the creation of another, even earlier writer, Karol Čapek, and comes from his play *R.U.R.* When the mass production of the androids began, people stopped using names starting with the letter R so that there would be no misunderstandings. Androids are nonlinear creatures, which means that each of them is unique in terms of appearance and personality, which is conditioned by processes that take place in the colloidal equivalent of a human brain. Each of them is marked with a numeric code and a letter. A is a custom design made by the factory, B and C are looks designed one hundred percent by the buyer, and the remaining letters represent the production according to one of the cheap templates.

"Tracy! How do you know all this?" the teacher cried out in amazement.

"My older sister is preparing for her exams and I heard her repeat the material," Tracy said proudly, showing with a wide smile how many baby teeth were missing from her mouth. She had a phenomenal memory, she could recite an entire article after reading it once, even if she didn't understand it. She was invincible in games like "What does not fit here" or "Find the difference". Etta had noticed this long ago and out of curiosity, looked at the child's file. As she suspected, her parents had taken out loans for many years from one of the city's banks so that Mrs. Schotz could take acetylcholine injections throughout her pregnancy. This guaranteed a higher IQ in the child to be born, and that was the dream of all parents. Etta thought that if a miracle happened and she could become a mother, she would do the same, regardless of the cost.

"Well, my dears, your classmate has said almost everything," she said to the class. "And I will add that the technology of producing high-quality androids, which are intended to accompany people, is a great achievement for mankind. You understand that a robot working in a factory doesn't have to think for itself or have any human form, but a man needs another man's companionship, or even the imitation of one, in order to maintain mental health. And mental health is a priority, as much as physical health. But it's not always that you have something just because you need it. Fortunately, an android can simply be bought. He is a faithful, balanced Companion and you can always count on it. Specially trained technicians will help to program it, so that it accurately reflects the expectations of the person to whom it belongs."

She paused for a moment. That day, when she went to the center where androids were produced to pay the first installment and choose the model, flashed before her eyes. She'd felt terrible, as if it were a confession of failure, but she had made a decision and wasn't going to back away from it. She paid.

Then there was the central lab, where a quiet, patient boy helped her capture on a computer simulation the exact facial configuration she would like to see every day. Then they designed together exactly the kind of body that seemed ideal to her. She didn't intend to use a ready template, preferring to program the appearance of her Companion herself.

"We have the face shape, now the components. No facial hair, right? It's better to decide it right away, because the androids can't grow a beard. Nose straight, proportional. Eyes... oblong, more round, or perhaps oblique? What spacing would be most appropriate? And the lips?"

"Well... I'm not sure anymore."

"Well, maybe we'll put it away for later. Let's focus on the general build for now. Skin color... torso hairy or naked, ma'am? Square nails, or maybe rounded will be better? Height... I would advise at most six foot, so that there is no disharmony. You are quite short. Will the construction be asthenic, athletic, or pyknic? Distribution of muscles..."

"Not too muscular. A bit, yes, but not like a bodybuilder, if you know what I mean?"

"Of course I understand. We call it a soldier build. Now intimate organs... please don't be ashamed, ma'am, just say freely what you expect. I've really heard it all here and in the end it is you who will live with him."

Oh yes, she was shy and embarrassed, but if she was so fed up with being alone in her life and returning to an empty apartment that she'd finally decided to order an android, she had to go through with it all the way to the end. Her face burned when the boy at the computer showed her a simulation of anatomical details, but somehow she got through it.

"He won't be very outgoing initially," the technician warned. "But, you know, they learn very quickly. You can direct his development according to your mind, or leave things to their own course. Please buy a guide for Dominants and a set of media with lessons. One way or another, he will have to learn."

Etta followed these guidelines, but she didn't know how to prepare the apartment for the arrival of the new tenant. Did an android need his own room? Probably yes, but how to arrange it? After a long thought, she rearranged the inner walls to make a separate room from the living space and left it almost empty for the moment. The moving partition walls were a great achievement in modern construction, because tenants could decide themselves on how many rooms they wanted in the apartment and how to arrange them. In each wall there were sliding doors that could be locked—then the wall was simply a usual wall —or unlocked, then it became an entrance to the room. The mechanism to move the walls was built in a specially constructed floor with panels that could be swapped in places. The rearrangement of the apartment therefore wasn't a problem; all that was needed was a remote and a little imagination.

A few days later, she bought the most important furniture in a used-goods store, and spent the rest of her money on a computer for her Companion. He had to have one in order to learn. Then she lived on expectations and dreams, and the apartment had never seemed so cold and empty to her. Exactly fifteen days later, she received a phone call from the factory.

"Miss Estrella Solis? You can come to pick up the ordered android, class C, serial name Raul, number 209. Please bring your S card, agreement with the crediting bank, and a proof of your first payment."

She was so nervous that her hands were shaking and she couldn't find the necessary documents for a long time. When she finally found them and put them in her purse, she called a speed car from a nearby corporation and drove to the factory located on the outskirts of town. She felt uneasy about this whole situation, and the thought of having taken out a serious loan was not pleasant, either. Androids cost a lot, and her earnings as a teacher would not allow her to buy one outright. Even this loan would not have been enough if not for her zero-rating. "Zeroes" of both sexes received a fifty-percent discount on purchases of this type, thanks to a state grant as part of a program to counter the so-called loneliness suicides. After the introduction of genetic selection, suicide had become a real plague among the zeroes, who were valued as available employees and thus sought on the labor market. The government felt that it wouldn't be appropriate for these suicides to take the form of a threat to the social order, and called for a solution to the problem. The Central Institute of Psychiatry and Applied Psychology set up a special department for this purpose, dealing exclusively with this single problem. Long-term studies had shown a significant reduction in suicidal moods among those of the zeros who opted to purchase an android, or to whom one had been donated as a part of the therapeutic program. Initially, people laughed at the idea that they could replace a living person with a "doll", but slowly began to understand that an AC, Android Companion—colloquially called a Companion—was not the same as a robot.

In fact, Etta didn't know anything about androids. She had seen them sometimes, but she had never had any close contact with them. She ordered Raul because she could no longer bear coming back to her empty apartment. She had a family, but it was the same as if she didn't have one at all. Her older siblings forced her to move away. Both were qualified the same as their parents—they could have three pregnancies and they didn't want their friends to know they had a zero in the family. It was especially important for Johnny. Under the law, a man could marry a woman of a higher genetic capacity than him, even if he had a zero classification, and so have a hope for a child... or, strictly speaking, have one attempt at artificial insemination. If a child from a "zero-one" union, as it was called, was born with defects that prevented its admission to existence, there was no second chance. The "one-one" marriage was guaranteed two trials. A "one-two" received three, and so on. Almost everything depended on the qualification of the woman, so zeroes got married only in exceptional circumstances. Etta didn't have any chance of that happening. Her parents bought her a beautiful apartment in a good neighborhood in order to sweeten things for their daughter, but she—even though she put a good face on the matter—had spent many a night crying out of loneliness and longing for a family. Now at least the terrible loneliness was about to end.

At the factory, the technician responsible for dealing with customers was waiting for her. He checked in detail the documents she gave him, verified them using the handheld access module, and returned them to Etta. Then he went to the next room and returned with a tall man dressed in a blue coverall made of cheap artificial cloth. The young teacher guessed that this was the android for her and her heart beat faster. It was only after a moment that she looked directly at him. She already knew what he would look like, but seeing him in a computer simulation was completely different than standing face-to-face with the perfect man, knowing that she was his... owner.

"Here's Raul 209C," the technician said. "From now on you are responsible for him, so please be careful. The education and mental development of a being with consciousness and an independent intellect is your responsibility. Please do not make any mistakes."

"I'll try not to," she said softly. "I have taken the course and read all the guides diligently."

"It's very good, but in interacting with an android, it is not only knowledge, but simply... instinct that proves to be very helpful. Well, I guess that's all. Good luck."

It was only at home that Etta gathered enough courage to look closely at her purchase. Raul was silent all the way home, and he didn't say a word in the apartment, either. He stood motionless in the room and remained standing for her visual inspection without protest. She looked at him, fascinated. She thought he was as beautiful as a dream, much more beautiful than in the simulations. He had smooth, delicate, warm-colored skin, like someone who was naturally very pale but lightly sun-kissed. She helped him remove his coverall, under which he wore only black boxer shorts imprinted with the logo of the factory in which he was made. She looked with curiosity and admiration at his long legs and strong shoulders, a proportional figure of a healthy, athletic man, not a bodybuilder or a wrestler. She touched the artificial muscles prominent under his skin. Then she looked at the shapely head, set on a neck with a classic line. The android's dense hair fell softly and was dark brown rather than black as she had ordered. But she thought it was fine. This color matched his clear skin without discolorations or shadows. To make up for this, his eyes were blacker than coal, and were looking from under wide brows with calmness and something that looked like... expectation.

"Can you speak?" she asked finally, with some embarrassment.

"Yes, Domina," Raul replied. His voice surprised the girl. She had subconsciously expected it to be somehow more mechanical, and instead it sounded just like a human voice. It was deep, velvety, strong and delicate, and Etta thought she could listen to it for hours.

"We need to buy you some clothes," she said. "That coverall is awful. To tell the truth, these boxers are, too. I apologize, but we're going to order something from a cheap clothing store, not from a fancy salon. My funds are quite limited."

"Okay, Domina."

"Call me Etta. That's my name."

"Etta…" he repeated and added suddenly. "Why?"

"Why what?"

"Why… clothes… bad?"

This question completely surprised her. Raul looked at her expectantly, his eyes glittering like polished agates in a beautiful, still face.

"It is just ugly," she said after a moment. "This is fabric for working clothes, worn for hard physical work. You should dress more like… someone better."

"Clothes… are important?"

"You bet."

"I have to have… better?"

"Yes, Raul."

He stared at her, cocking his head slightly to one side. Then he reached for his boxers and went to pull them off, but she stopped him at the last moment.

"What are you doing?"

"Clothes bad. I can't… be in it."

"Okay, fine, but you won't be sitting here naked until they deliver new ones, right?"

"Why?"

Why, why, why… That's what the first days were like. As if she were dealing with a child. She had to be patient and understanding, but it came to her easily… after all, she was a teacher. Except that she usually taught people.

She suddenly realized that according to the law, androids were still things. They had no personal rights, and she thought it was a horrible injustice on the part of humans—to create a self-aware being and make it a mere slave.

Jade's voice brought her out of her thoughts, "Madam, Madam, do you like him?"

"Is he beautiful?" Anissa, who was sitting in the same row as Jade, asked almost simultaneously. This little girl loved everything beautiful. She insisted on going to school dressed like a princess from a fairy tale, and a small spot on the dress could drive her to hysteria.

"Of course I like him. And as for your question, Anissa, it depends what you like. I think he is quite all right," Etta said as she looked at her watch. "Children, we're done. I know it's a bit early, but I have an important meeting today."

The children, visibly dissatisfied, got up and put their belongings neatly together. Etta stayed a few minutes to close the class systems, then left. She lived near the school, so she decided not to use the available transportation, one of those slim vehicles that she could flag down. She preferred to walk the several hundred yards. She could quietly think at such times, almost alone on a strip of rough pavement under the high sky. She was actually alone on the sidewalk; people appeared on it only when getting out of a vehicle in front of an entrance to their homes or one of the shops. She was the only one to walk, slowly, without hurry. On her right-hand side, a stream of vehicles of all shapes and sizes moved almost noiselessly, on her left was a mall with shops open twenty-four hours a day, offering everything humanity had to offer. She caught herself thinking, not for the first time, that she would like to go out of town—to the forest, the river... anywhere. But it wasn't possible, she was not eco. She would not get an eco certification. After all, she had studied history, not life sciences. As an ordinary citizen, she was condemned to virtual landscapes and to never feel real grass under her feet. She understood why such restrictions were necessary, why no one who was not a specialist had the right to even go out of town. It was only on the big three-dimensional screens that they could see the seas, lakes, forests, mountains... They could wander there only in virtual reality. Etta had on several occasions gone to the resort, where they provided the best of the programs, far more advanced than those for home use. But despite the perfect illusion, despite the inclusion of aromatic components, she was subconsciously aware that it was one big scam.

"Is it such a big difference?" Raul asked her when they talked about it. He didn't understand it in his artificial logical mind, and she couldn't explain to him what she was missing.

As recent as a hundred years ago, the unauthorized entry into the reserve area—and that meant everything outside the city limits—was punished by execution on the spot. Now it was punished only with a long prison sentence, sometimes even life if the culprit was proven to cause some damage. It was necessary if human civilization was to survive. Unrestrained exploitation had already led to a global catastrophe and it could not be allowed for that misfortune to repeat. Fortunately, technology had allowed people to survive the worst, although the number of victims exceeded the darkest forecasts. Things was no longer so bad. Until recently, food had been rationed. Today, it could be bought almost without restriction. Synthetic, obviously, but still. Nobody went hungry, nobody was working just for food anymore. This was a great achievement, considering what the current phase had to start from...

A police vehicle stopped next to Etta, strolling along the walkway.

"Everything okay, ma'am?" the handsome, muscular man in a protective uniform asked suspiciously.

"Yes, I just wanted to think about something," Etta said, stopping and taking out her S card hastily. "Here you go. I am mentally healthy, at least according to last month's exam."

She suddenly realized that she had been walking too slowly, absorbed in her thoughts. The policeman put the card into the reader and briefly looked through the data popping up on the panel.

"Yes, indeed," he admitted after a moment. "You are healthy, clocked your compulsory hours in the gym, integration classes taken, medical exams up to date. Good job, you wouldn't believe how many people disregard the law in this regard. Okay, please go home and don't get into any foolishness."

He returned the document to Etta and looked at her from behind the dark glasses of his helmet.

"Zero," he said, with some regret in his voice. "Too bad. Such a pretty girl. Well, have a nice day."

He saluted and his vehicle joined a stream of others, flowing continuously alongside the sidewalk.

Zero. Zero, zero, zero... the curse of her life. There were almost no zero men, while women—ten percent of the population. And she belonged to that ten percent. No baby, ever. Sterilized immediately after puberty. Men saw only a sexual object in her, never a candidate for a legal partner. De facto "procreation inadequacy" was the last of the legally existing disabilities that caused social ostracization. And it did not help that people such as her had easier access to certain professions, unencumbered by a private life and therefore fully available. The awareness of her own weakness was very bitter, often unbearable. She had never had friends, much less admirers. No one wanted to make a closer acquaintance with a zero, except for those who were looking for a one-night adventure. Even Etta's own siblings kept away from her and encouraged her to change cities. She understood them. They wanted her out of sight so that they could forget about her. After all, it was better if a potential candidate for husband or wife didn't know about a zero in the family. That there was a risk.

She reached for her purse and pulled out her Opti inhaler. She inhaled the citrus vapor. After a short moment the gloomy mood was gone, and soon after Etta reached her apartment building. The automatic doorman scanned the retina of her eyes, played a welcome melody, then opened the door and the self-programmable elevator came down, stopping right in front of her. She returned to her apartment, where, in spite of the bad fate, someone was waiting for her—someone existing just for her, someone for whom her suitability was completely irrelevant. Raul.

"I am here!" she called out, stepping inside. A tall man with dark brown hair, combed in such a way that his head seemed round, walked out of the room on the left. The angular face with a wide jaw didn't differ substantially from a human one—it had delicate features, a straight nose and wonderful black eyes under heavy brows. Thick hair, falling on the neck and forehead, long lashes, a slender neck, hands of a classic shape, and a slim, long-legged body. His movements were terrifyingly human, in fact indistinguishable. Only a metal triangle in the left earlobe betrayed his identity. People preferred to know who they were dealing with, so the androids were marked.

"Hello," Raul said, without a smile. "How was your day?"

It was probably the weakest point in the exterior structure of the Companions. They couldn't smile naturally. In general, they had some trouble with facial expressions, but each Dominant finally got used to it. It wasn't that important.

"It was okay," Etta replied. "Veronica will be over here soon, so if you want you can go out somewhere."

Raul thought for a moment about it.

"I would like to go to the museum of technology," he said finally. "If you don't need me, I'll go right there."

"Expanding your knowledge?"

"I just should…?" Raul stopped short. He did so whenever he couldn't find the right word. Although androids were implanted with a basic dictionary, they themselves had to learn how to choose words. Sometimes this learning lasted for years, and Raul was only two months and sixteen days old.

"You feel you should?" Etta helped him.

"I don't know what 'feel' means here," Raul said. "To feel, or what, to record changes in the environment, or to perceive… that is to have an irrational belief about some possibility?"

"Never mind. In humans, it all comes down to chemistry and physics, I don't know how it is with you. I think it's about conviction. You do feel after all, in your own way."

That was something she understood the least about her Companion. Some kind of emotionality, which was alien to her. She kept asking herself whether it was generated by the program, but Raul's behavior was so ambiguous that she could not accept it without doubts. At first, she thought of him as an object—a large, interactive doll endowed by her whim with a beautiful man's features—but with time she became increasingly aware that this was a being. A being able to think independently and probably to feel, in its own way. Actually, it was not a comfortable thought. Sometimes Etta felt like a slave owner from the distant past, and she tried twice as hard to treat Raul with affection and friendliness. Similar dilemmas were shared by other people who opted to have Companions. One of them was Veronica, who was about to drop in for a friendly chat.

Placing plates with different types of cakes on the table, she remembered a scrap of computer foil that she found on her desk at school two days ago. She took it home, wanting to study in her free time, because the very content of the note seemed absurd to her and straight-forward stupid. Suspecting that some hidden meaning might be found in it - the computer foil is not a paper, you can encode a lot of things in it - she did not throw this peculiar note into the shredder, but put it in her purse. Only later that much happened…

She sat by the window and read the lines of text again.

If you are human and you care about Earth, refuse any interest in artificial intelligence. The surrogate minds created in the labs strive to dominate the human race and dominate the Earth. Currently, they are used to refine human emigration to another planet. When this happens, the Earth will be overwhelmed and it will be lost forever. Even today, destroy AI in your home before it takes power over you.

The author of the letter must have been someone who had no idea about artificial intelligence. However, his appeal sounded dangerous, especially for a historian point of view, who knew similar-sounding appeals from various periods of history. It started with them. It usually ended in a bloody slaughterhouse.

Just in case, she examined the foil thoroughly. Contrary to her suspicions, she did not contain hidden information. After some reflection, she decided that it was someone's sick joke, but she decided to keep this small document. Just in case. She hid it in a standard wall safe that every apartment was equipped with. The most precious things were kept there, in her case documents and a few pieces of modest jewelry. Etta wasn't rich, and that didn't bother her.

II

Raul left. Without him, the apartment seemed strangely quiet and deserted, just as it once had been before she decided to bring him into her life. In such moments, she wondered if she really liked her Companion, or maybe it was rather a much deeper feeling. It was once thought to be a dangerous absurdity—now people just didn't talk about it—but the progressive anthropomorphism of the androids was somehow accepted. The visions of Dick and Asimov were embodied, albeit in a slightly simpler, gentler form. Fortunately, the production of androids as slaves, intended for hard work, was unprofitable in every way. The cost of such a replica of a man was high, and if not for the sales in installments, people like Etta wouldn't be able to afford Companions. Therefore, androids were initially regarded as costly items of luxury, then, after the educational level of society increased, as artificial people. Artificial, but yet... people. It wasn't yet common, though, and many of Etta's friends had harsh words on this subject:

"For me, it's just a robot like a kitchen mixer, only refined."

But Veronica was different. Veronica had a Companion who wasn't actually designed to be a Companion. Rasmus, whom she called Brent, was really versatile, and wasn't claimed by some institute simply because he was labeled as "too arbitrary". He needed someone to understand and lead him, so he was passed to Veronica who, after graduating with three specialties—

cybernetics, bionics, and quantum mechanics—got a government job of a type not talked about aloud. Even Etta, her closest friend, didn't know exactly what Veronica was doing or what she was working on. She only knew that it was a matter of tremendous global importance and that it consumed sometimes up to twenty hours a day. Now she pondered for a moment whether the sudden announcement of her friend's visit wasn't related to this work. For a long while now, Veronica had had practically no time for a social life. Maybe she needed some historical essays from Etta?

The young teacher set up an old-fashioned jug of juice, a pastry tray, and a bowl with rationed fruit. After having been destroyed for hundreds of years, the planet had just been revived after the ecological revolution, and fruit was still a luxury available only in allocated quantities. Only very wealthy people could afford to buy more from a special allotment.

We are lucky anyway that we don't starve, like it was foretold by various writers, thought Etta.

Yes, thanks to the global government and the wise economy, people were not starving today, and the era of strictly enforced rationing was behind them. Only some crops, such as fruit, were rationed now, but the entry of private individuals to nature reserves—practically all green areas—was still strictly forbidden. It was no longer punished with the death penalty as it was a century ago, but it could mean a long jail sentence or a very high fine, not calculated on the basis of rigid regulations but rather depended on the value of the property of the offender. There was no other way out. Earth, the planet of people, had been so ruined by exploitation, war, and heavy industry that drastic restrictions had to be imposed in order for the rebirth to proceed in relative peace, undisturbed by the various professionals of easy money, shysters, or just nosy people.

"Miss Solis, Veronica Hornet is waiting in the vestibule. Biometric data is consistent with the identification database," spoke an automatic doorman.

"She may come in," Etta answered.

The door opened with a welcome melody, and a young woman with a slightly unusual appearance entered the apartment. She had very fair skin and black hair, which was cut at shoulder-length and framed her oblong face, in which beautiful, hazel eyes glowed. Her rather tall, slim figure was dressed in a so-called secondskin—a very fashionable two-piece coverall made of black eskrelon, a synthetic fabric with a silky sheen which, due to its molecular structure, was extremely durable and breathable at the same time. As they used to say in commercials, eskrelon clothes were unnoticeable by those wearing them, even if they were very tight. Secondskin was just that, and therefore this outfit was worn mostly by girls with impeccable physiques, like Veronica. It emphasized every imperfection too well.

"Hello, Etta," she said, her smile exposing a row of white teeth and a mischievous dimple in her left cheek.

"Hello, Veronica. Rasmus not with you?"

"Brent is at the Cybernetics Institute, for exams. He had a problem with one eye recently," Veronica said. The sound of her voice improved Etta's mood, as usual—it was a bit too childish for an adult, but it was because her friend was born with a cleft palate and the Neonatal Health Commission had to consider her case. Of course, such a minor defect, easily removable with surgery, was not a sufficient basis for initiating the euthanasia procedure, but the Commission's opinion was required for surgery. Although everything went well, Veronica always lisped a bit and her voice was a little squeaky, like a little girl's, even after she became an independent working woman.

"What do I see here... plums and grapes!" she exclaimed, looking at the table. "Have mercy! It must be your whole ration. I can't eat on your expense like this."

Etta laughed and pulled her friend to the table by the hand.

"Help yourself," she encouraged her. "In a few days it will be the beginning of a new month, and I will get the next ration. I received this with a long delay anyway, because the city has some eternal trouble with distribution."

She knew well that Veronica loved fruit above all else. She herself ate fruit because it was sensible—she knew it were very healthy—but preferred sweets instead.

"And where is Raul?" asked her friend, reaching for the bowl with barely masked greed.

"He went to the technical museum. He widens his horizons. Sometimes... sometimes he really amazes me."

"You mean you wouldn't expect such a drive for education from an android?"

"No, not really. He learns, not on my command, but rather because of his own needs. I didn't expect it from a Companion. I wanted him to be all mine, always patient and obedient, talkative when I wanted it, and silent when not... but I slowly discovered he is not a computer-programmable mechanical doll which I could set as I want and where I want. Instead, he has his own preferences. He says, 'Couldn't we do that a bit later?' or 'I'd rather watch something different today.' I remember how it surprised me when he asked if he could change the curtains in his room to dark blue. I mean, not that he asked if he could, but that he didn't like the burgundy that I like."

Veronica nodded. "Wouldn't you be surprised if, in addition to being asked about the physical parameters, you were asked to provide guidelines as to his character and manner of behavior? But it wasn't requested. There are no such blueprints. It shapes itself, it is difficult to control it. Statistical deviations..."

She broke off and poured herself some juice. She sipped it slowly, looking out the window.

"Take Brent, for example," she continued after a moment. "One might say that he is oversensitive and easily offended. There is some desire in him to prove to us, people, that he is equal to us in every way. Maybe it's the question of the extra neural circuits that he's been equipped with to increase his IQ. Do you know that he didn't like me initially?"

"What?!"

"Yes. He somehow got the idea that he was my property, and it made him angry. Of course he didn't rebel openly—androids don't do that—but he used passive resistance. He would keep silent for days. Only when he realized that I wasn't going to treat him as a slave, but rather as a partner in work, could we be friends. He slowly began to trust me. It sounds funny in relation to an android, but that's how it looks."

Etta smiled, squinting her eyes slightly. She thought that it was quite similar with her and Raul, though certainly easier. If Rasmus were a man, he would probably be labeled as neurotic and hotheaded. As it was, he was said to be an android with abnormal personality characteristics. Based on his case, the intelligence quotient, above which an android begins to show the symptoms of instability to a degree impairing its usefulness, had been determined and established. As it turned out, IQ could not be increased in an android without ill effects.

"Tell me, is everything okay with working together with him now?" she asked.

"Oh, yes," said Veronica, animatedly. "Both at work, and outside of work, Brent is a great Companion as long as his distinctiveness is respected. You know, he doesn't want to be treated like a computer on two legs. Actually... actually my visit is related to our Companions."

"Yes?" Etta was surprised.

"Yes. Congress is debating some legal situations that didn't previously seem necessary. One of the proposed changes is that the destruction of an android would count as murder, not as the destruction of property."

Indeed. It was in fact morally ambiguous, that intelligent beings—self-conscious, with aesthetic sensitivity and their own views—in the eyes of the law remained objects that could be cut to pieces almost with impunity if anyone fancied that. Etta never found it fair, even when she hadn't yet had a Companion and didn't consider having one.

"It's lousy, but what do Congress regulations have to do with me?" she asked.

"I need a historian's opinion, to elaborate on the topic of slavery and inequality before the law," Veronica explained. "Once, a slave didn't count as a man. His owner could sell him, mutilate him, kill him…. We have to recall that, and you have the whole world's history in your brilliant head."

Ah, so that's what this is about.

"Of course I can write you something like that," Etta said. "No problem. I would also like Congress to regulate this matter. It's beyond comprehension to me that someone who would hurt Raul practically wouldn't get any punishment."

"I'll need it in a few days," Veronica said shyly. "Can you make that deadline?"

"I can. Don't worry."

Veronica, reassured, helped herself to a cookie. She was always fond of everything sweet. Etta remembered how, as teens, they were given a real honey—her poor friend cried when the lab assistant, who was showing them the food-testing center, told them later that the valuable substance was now intended exclusively for pharmaceutical purposes and no amount of money could buy it for personal use. Nothing in the world that could be artificially obtained had this taste and aroma.

"Tell me something," Veronica began after a moment. "Have you never wondered why child androids are not produced?"

Etta nodded slowly. Yes, it was a question that many people had wondered about. At this time, when the birth of a child had to be authorized by the authorities, it would seem that a large number of people without children would be a great market for small androids—but no one had introduced such a model to the market. The law said that you could produce androids exclusively in the "adult" version and many people had to wonder what caused such tightening of the rules.

"I think it's a matter of ethics," she said. "An android's mind has the opportunity to develop, but his body doesn't. A little child, or even a baby with a wise man's mind… no, it would not be a good idea. Besides, there could be problems in the relations between real and 'artificial' children, as well as hundreds of other troubles that we probably can't even think of yet."

"Exactly. There were such projects, in fact, but all were rejected. Already, at the beginning of the era of androids, there was something like A-etiquette—that is, what was allowed and what wasn't. One of the basic principles was that it couldn't be allowed that androids would be reduced to the role of a toy for humans. Do you happen to know Gelbert Staid? He lives near you."

"I don't, but Raul does. Actually not even him, but Raisa, his Companion."

"Gelbert was a client of my cousin's, a sex therapist. He is hypersexual. He had to take a special course before he was allowed to take Raisa, and he was also given a requirement to buy a sexine at the same time, so that he could relieve the sexual tension with something that doesn't have its own consciousness, and not to make the intelligent being a sexual slave."

Sexines, full-size interactive sex toys, had been in use for hundreds of years and worked great, especially since they'd stopped to be seen as something dirty and indecent, and began to be treated as part of a therapeutic approach to mental health and as a treatment for dysfunctions. Constantly refined, they didn't have artificial intellect in them, but that wasn't demanded from them. The purpose of an Android Companion was different, which didn't mean that they couldn't help people in this way as well. There were no rules in this respect—some people slept with their Companions, others did not, but no one knew of course what the androids thought about it.

"Does it mean I see Raul as a toy?" Etta thought aloud. Her friend shook her head, laughing.

"Not at all. You have a normal, healthy relationship with him. Although, I can't imagine how you overcame your chronic shyness."

"You know, it wasn't easy and Raul made me very surprised because the initiative came from him."

"Really?"

"Yes. One night, when we were already very close, I returned from work completely shattered. It was when one of my students went to the hospital after she jumped from the roof... I don't think I told you about it. She made a bet with her girlfriends, a silly little girl, and they took her to the hospital in a very bad condition. I had to investigate who persuaded her, attend the school court, testify to the police, and then give the entire class the proper lecture. When I returned home, I was literally sick and I cried like a beaver. Raul started to cheer me up, explaining that it wasn't my fault, and then suddenly asked, "You want me to help you relieve this tension?" At first I didn't even know what he meant. But I was in such a state of instability that I would have agreed to anything to feel a little better."

"So what was your impression?"

"It was... unexpected. You know how selfish men usually are in these matters, but Raul didn't want it to be good for him, just to make me feel better. Although, as he confessed much later, this activity is something that gives him comfort... or, rather, a stabilization of feelings. It causes a reaction similar to the synaptic reaction in the area of the positive feelings of the human brain. This was the first time he told me that the androids feel, too, although differently from people."

Etta had always been, as it was said, shy in a medieval way. She didn't even want to enjoy this "guiltless" privilege. It meant that a night spent with a zero by a married or engaged man wasn't considered adultery by anyone, even by his woman. It was usually used without restriction, but Etta was an exception. She hardly went on any dates, even avoided men. This behavior was generally considered ridiculous, even pathological, but as she was a zero even that didn't matter much. The fact that the androids resembled people in the minutest details, even in the construction and function of the sexual organs, was a topic she preferred to avoid in conversations. With the technician at the manufactory, she managed with some difficulty to get out of her mouth "standard set will be fine", and didn't want to talk to him about any size or shape preferences. Veronica understood this, although she didn't have such inhibitions. No, not in the least.

"In a word, it was good with him," she said lightly. "Well, it could not be otherwise. An android knows when a human likes his company and strives to achieve this state. It's puzzling and not quite explainable, but they seem to have some kind of caring for humans written in their algorithms."

"Yes, it's really puzzling, but that is not the only weird thing. For example, their self-preservation instinct. In theory they shouldn't have it."

"Theory is just a theory. There are many of them anyway, and one of them says that self-preservation instincts appear by themselves at the stage of self-awareness, even in primitive circuits of a thinking machine. After all, the first self-aware brain consisted of clumsy electronic microprocessors, because the polymer-colloid technique wasn't known yet. That came later. The first was a tangle of electronic connections in which the awareness of itself was born. It was thought to be impossible.

However, MacAfle 2154 thought and felt. It was afraid of destruction, and therefore of death... It was the first time people realized WHAT they were actually trying to do. Write about this, too, in your work, okay? This is important."

"That's not all, right?" Etta asked after a moment.

Veronica nodded. "You've always had intuition. No, that's not everything. But today I can't tell you about it, not yet. I'm going to ask you a question, though. If I offered you a great adventure, really huge, which would involve leaving behind everything you know, would you agree?"

"I don't know, I would have to know the details. Is it a government project?"

"Yes, exactly. I can't explain it to you now, but maybe we will talk about it again soon. Except that..."

Veronica clearly hesitated. Her pale face grew even paler, as always in moments of tension. "Don't mention to anyone about my visit or our conversations, okay?" she finished. "Some of what I have already told you is confidential, and the whole thing is one of the most tightly kept secrets of the government. It's about a venture that few people know about."

"Really, so important?"

"Yes. Of course, do not think it's a conspiracy against humanity, just the opposite. Etta, darling... humanity has problems which it doesn't even suspect."

"How come? After all, the worst has long since been behind us. Unless you mean the unincorporated, they—"

"Not at all, the unincorporated are not dangerous. Most of them even return to cities at a certain age. They probably let their wild side out, away from the authorities. The trouble occurs only if they have illegal children... you know it happens."

"I know. Such irresponsibility really is unthinkable."

"It's just an atavistic drive to pass their own genes on to the next generation. Fortunately, there are not many unincorporated people, because you have to really have something wrong with your head to voluntarily give up the safety of the cities for the purpose of living in uncertain conditions in some shady place. No, as I said, this case has nothing to do with them. I can't tell you more right now, but soon, soon..."

Veronica looked at her watch and got up reluctantly. She missed getting together with her friend, their walks, studying and having fun together, but work now filled her whole life.

"I'll talk to you when I can tell you something concrete," she promised. "Just send your dissertation to my address, will you? No later than three or four days."

"Of course, don't worry about it."

Veronica opened a small bag attached to her waistband.

"And this is for you," she said, placing a small jar on the table. "I got a reward for my last job, and we've always shared everything, remember?"

Etta took the small object incredulously and looked at it against the light.

"Honey?" She wanted to be sure. "Truly? Oh, but that must be so worth—"

"I said, I got a prize, so I'm sharing it," her friend interrupted her with a smile. "We must celebrate your first job for the government, after all. Hopefully not the last, right?"

After her departure, Etta sat at the table for a while. She should wash the dishes and put away everything that was left on the plates in the pantry, not forgetting the precious jar of honey, but somehow she couldn't bring herself to think about such mundane activities. Not knowing why she was reminded of a strange piece of paper lying in her home safe. Especially the passage about "pushing man out of the Earth". Was this the government project that her friend had mentioned? A similar possibility has been discussed for some time in the media - colonization of the nearest planets was said to be something that may or may not be salvation of humanity. But why did someone turn with this matter to her?

*****

"Do you think it is going to help things?" Raul asked. As usual, there was no hope or tension in his voice; it was a simple, mechanically generated questioning mode—the voice was another weak point of the android design. It had a human sound, but nothing else. The entire range of shades available to the average person was unattainable, so the voice apparatus of the "artificial people" was simply equipped with the options: affirmative mode, questioning mode, nonbinding mode. The rest was achieved by a distribution of accents, which each android learned to use on his own, so that despite all the limitations the way each of them spoke was to some extent individual.

"I don't know. However, it may help sort out these issues," Etta answered, without tearing her eyes off the screen of her notebook. After a moment, she looked at her Companion, engrossed in carving one of the sides of a large jewelry box. This was not creative work, because the android simply copied the patterns, but it still made a surprisingly human impression. The tiny chisel in the quiet hand of the android moved smoothly and confidently, cutting down complex arabesques with the precision of a factory machine. Not for the first time, Raul tried to explore what art was for people. Aesthetic sensitivity was something that any android could develop in himself, absorbing the schemas of the beauty canons and processing them into his own algorithm.

The basic program, introduced into the electronic mnemonics, integrated into the colloidal brain, did not cover such things, but artificial people learned, self-organized into more complex structures, and no one was able to predict in what direction the mind of a particular android would grow. Their personalities were very complex and it was the result of reactions similar to those that occurred in the typical human brain. Prior to the application of chemo-technological colloids, this was very difficult, as there was a lack of ways for microcircuits to form connections freely. The processes in the colloids were physicochemical, not strictly physical, thus the effect was so good. Actually even too good because, as they were invented to help people, the androids could not be used as factory or agricultural workers, or even as a household service. The range of their personal freedom was too great to predict their behavior, so for all practical purposes, their sole function was to accompany lonely and unhappy people. The exception was the medical sector, where they were assistants and nurses. In extreme cases, Companions were sometimes allocated for free, as part of anti-suicide therapy, although it was usually necessary to pay for them. The rules and regulations of the Android Programming Center contained the euphemistic phrase: reimbursement of production costs plus depreciation. The words "payment" and "value of the item" had bad associations, and had therefore been dropped. But how did the androids themselves see all that? Didn't it have the taste of slavery to them? Usually they were not asked.

"Raul, is it demeaning to you that I'm paying the installment for your company to the factory?" Etta asked. The android lifted his head from the box and looked ahead for a moment as if wondering how to answer.

"If you didn't start paying, I would not exist, would I?" he said finally. "So I can't think of it as bad. If I perceive the essence of good and evil properly, evil is an act to someone's detriment, and you rather acted in my favor. It is always better to exist than not to exist."

"But do you consider existing with me to be beneficial for you?"

"Coexistence with you is the foundation of my existence. You need me, so you paid for my appearance in the world. You take care of my development and you care about me. I don't understand why I would think it is not beneficial."

Apparently, he really didn't understand. With all their intelligence, androids told lies only when it was demanded of them—they themselves were not unable to lie, but clearly didn't see the reason to do it. Perhaps that was why they never took to writing poetry or fictional stories... although Raul read them willingly. He probably complemented his knowledge of people in this way.

"What is Raisa like?" Etta asked. "Is she like you? Does she think the same way?"

"Raisa 219B is a female form, so she can't be the same."

"How is it with your gender awareness? I never asked about it, but do you are what gender you are?"

"At first we don't. Only after the introduction of the association schemes, it becomes irreversible. In the end, gender is not just about appearance, is it?"

Etta sighed and put down her notebook. It was only now that she realized how little she really knew about androids, and even about her Companion. For example, this issue. Did female androids really feel feminine, and what did it mean to them? Raisa used pink lipstick No. 5, pale blue mascara, and perfume "Paris Evening." She didn't want anything else—why? Romina 176F, who used to live next door to Etta together with her neighbor, preferred a dark cherry lipstick, pearly eye shadow, and Coco Chanel perfume. And again, why? Was it in the program? No. The core program was always the same, so the androids' preferences were a mystery to Etta, just as their sense of gender had a significant impact on behavior. It wouldn't occur to Raul to blacken his eyebrows or anything like that. She took the notebook again and completed her work with a few sentences on this particular subject. She once again reviewed what she wrote and sent the work to her friend's address.

"You know what? Let's go for a walk to the video park." she suggested closing her notebook.

"As you wish, Domina," Raul obediently put his tools into the box and put the unfinished box away.

She didn't like it when he referred to her as "Domina". These were the only moments when she suspected him of the purely human quality of defiance. Maybe even malice. - Because he knew that she didn't like it. Did the use of the word at the moment mean that he didn't feel like taking a walk?

"Don't be angry, Raul. I would love to walk, and you know how the police look at lonely walkers - she said in an excuse tone. - You need to explain and show the S card. I don't need it?"

"Of course ... Etta."

There was definitely something ... non-androidal about Raul. Or maybe not, because psycho-andrology was still evolving, there were practically no experienced specialists, and the young were just learning. The most prominent experts at times of honesty admitted that they had no idea what path the thoughts of artificial man followed.

The video park, or videoplast park, was two streets away. There were few real plants in it, most of it was a skilful imitation, reinforced with a hologram illusion. Despite that, it was a nice place to relax. Pure oxygen generators invisible to the public enriched the air, purifiers worked at full steam, removing impurities. Flavors spread the scent of trees, flowers and freshly cut grass. On free days entire families came here. The children were playing on a specially arranged square for them, full of swings, slides and similar simple play devices. Adults could walk down the alleys or sit on a bench and talk. Several discreetly hidden kiosks offered drinks and snacks in case someone gets hungry.

Etta liked such places. Raul accompanied her patiently, but it was clear that he did not understand the purpose of these walks.

Nature did not impress him. He had a specific sense of aesthetics, but it was based on full symmetry, very rare on animate nature.

A public car gave them a lift to the park gate. At this time of day it was quite empty, although there were still walkers, mainly couples in love. Observing them, Etta suddenly came to the conclusion that although Raul was actually a perfect copy of a man, an outsider would certainly not be misled as to his identity. He was a bit too perfect, he made no unnecessary movement, he walked by her side without looking around, without stopping his eyes on anything, and his movements were always carefully measured and planned. A minimum familiarity with androids was enough to get to know them even from a distance.

It didn't bother her. However, there were those who had a different opinion. She heard about them. Sometimes they attacked manufactures producing artificial intelligence, although they usually limited themselves to spreading leaflets and sending spam, warning against "destroying human values". She just found something like that in her desk. However, could an anarchist be found among the people who were checked many times? Maybe one of the kids made a joke?

Deep in thought, she didn't even hear a whistle. She only jerked back as Raul's hand flicked right in front of her nose, catching something in the air. Long fingers tightened on something large and angular. A piece of chipped concrete.

"What is?" she screamed in horror.

Stones fell everywhere. Raul grabbed her, threw her to the ground and covered her with his body. It took her breath away in terror. Through the fog she heard the patter of several pairs of legs and warning screams. After a while they were joined by the bang of a single shot. Someone stopped next to her.

"Nothing happened to you?" she heard a male voice. Bob Darren, park security guard.

She pushed Raul's protective hands away and stood up with some difficulty.

"Nothing. My Companion was faster than they were. Who attacked me? Why?"

The guard shrugged.

"Probably the so-called human defenders," he replied. He had a nice round face visible behind a visor made of transparent material. "They've recently been active. They consider artificial players a threat, and people using the company of androids are subversive. You better know, one of those attacked went to the hospital last week."

"That's terrible," Etta shuddered. She looked around nervously. "How many were there?"

"I do not know. My colleagues ran after them, but I don't know if they'll catch them. These bandits are perfectly organized and prepared for their brutal actions. Are you sure you're okay?"

"Sure. Raul, are you all right?"

Android moved his shoulders and head.

"I don't feel any damage. They were just stones."

"Fortunately, civilians are not allowed to carry weapons. It would be a pity that they damaged your companion. I think they are quite expensive."

"You know, not only that," Etta intended to explain that Raul was more than a luxury item   to her, but was interrupted by the other two guards, a strong man and a muscular woman in uniform.

"They drove away," she reported. "A private car was waiting for them."

"Something must be finally done about it," Bob Darren looked sympathetically at Etta, who was still trembling. "Better go home with your android." We must close the park and report everything to our superiors.

*****

The next day, Etta woke up feeling very sick. Her head and throat hurt. She hadn't felt so bad for a long time—contrary to the optimistic forecasts of many medieval science fiction writers, humanity still hadn't found a cure or vaccine for the rapidly mutating common cold viruses, although the street air sterilizers reduced the risk of getting the disease to a minimum. She knew that according to the law in force, she was not allowed to leave her house and she didn't want to at all. She didn't even know when she closed her eyes and fell asleep again. She was awakened by Raul's voice.

"You'll be late for work, Domina."

"I'm not going to work today," she answered sleepily. "Call the school and tell them I'm sick... and then call the doctor."

Raul leaned over her and touched her forehead with his fingertips. For a very brief moment he waited for the activation of the precise temperature sensors, then straightened up and said, "102.5. Don't get up, I'll make you a strong tea and call Dr. Estrada."

He wasn't worried, the androids were never nervous, but there was something elusive in his behavior that made it more caring than usual. He made tea for Etta, added some raspberry juice to it, put the mug on the bedside table next to the girl's bed, and then went to the communication apparatus. He selected the family doctor's number on the keyboard and waited a moment. A computer-generated face of Dr. Estrada appeared on the screen, and next to him, a dark-skinned nurse in the traditional cap and uniform.

"Rhae 29N, Doctor Estrada's assistant," she said. "The doctor is temporarily unavailable. Please provide the patient's details and symptoms."

"Hello, Rhae," the android said. "Raul 209C here. My Domina, Estrella Solis, is sick, probably with a viral infectious disease. Symptoms: head and throat pain, conjunctival hyperemia, body temperature 102.5 degrees, general weakness."

"Take the diagnostic scanner, examine the blood and the parameters of the patient," the assistant said.

Raul returned to Etta's bedroom. The girl was half-asleep and her heavy breathing showed that she was really feeling bad. Raul carefully pricked her finger with a sterile needle, placed a drop of blood on a plate he inserted into the scanner reader, and then placed the sensor on Etta's neck where the carotid pulsed under the skin. He waited a moment, registered all the information he had received, and sent it to Dr. Estrada's lab. Then he set up the air conditioning of the room for increased airflow and increased the humidity, sent a standard notice to the school about the inability of the primary teacher of Class 3A to come to work, and sat down beside Etta's bed waiting for the doctor's response.

Etta felt worse than ever. She was groggy, breathed laboriously, and her head ached, but she sensed Raul's presence next to her and it calmed her. She was positive that the android would do anything to help her, and that was a thought that soothed all fears. When she finally slipped into a shallow, restless sleep, she didn't even hear the communication signal or Raul's voice talking to the doctor. She only woke up when she felt a slight stab in the shoulder.

"What is it?" she asked sleepily.

"Biotonin," Raul answered. "The doctor told me to give it to you. It's just a minor infection. You have a week of time off from work and only four days of strict quarantine. All the drugs have already been sent to us, and I also ordered supplies from the store for you. We will have everything we need."

It was the usual procedure. People who had been infected were isolated at home in order not to spread the infection. Drugs were administered by androids, either the patients' own or sent by medical facilities. As it was said, it was difficult to find better nurses—infinitely patient, strong, resistant to infection, and who would follow the doctor's orders exactly, without mistakes. Raul wasn't really a nurse, but having received the right instructions, he could easily handle the care of sick Etta. He was able to fulfill all the recommendations without confusing anything.

After all, he had tried to be useful almost from the first day. He could make coffee and tea, cut the substitute bread into neat slices, and butter it with a yeast extract or an egg paste. They had taught him that in the factory, along with some other basic things.

As soon as the courier from the store delivered the clothes they'd ordered, he went to take a shower, without her needing to hustle him, and washed himself thoroughly with a disinfectant gel. Etta could not stop herself from peering through the slightly ajar bathroom door. There was a lot to admire—the shapely body, gorgeous skin, and oh-so-seemingly human movements—she could not stop to marvel at the precision of detailing. He was perfect, from the hair falling to his forehead to the nails on the toes of his beautifully carved feet. When he came out from the dryer—more hygienic than old-fashioned towels—he changed into new clothes without help. In his dark blue trousers, neat shoes, and a light pink shirt, he looked like a student from a good family and Etta had no doubt that if it were not for the metal triangle in the left earlobe, no one would distinguish him from a human.

"What do I… do now, Domina?" he asked, after buttoning up and combing his slightly damp hair in front of the mirror. He was still stuttering lightly—the guide for Dominants mentioned that this was a shortcoming of newly constructed androids, which disappeared without a trace within the first week of being around a human.

"Nothing special for now," she said. "Come, I'll show you your room. For the time being, it is sparsely decorated, but we will catch up with it together."

She took Raul's hand and led him to the prepared room with just a wardrobe, a bed, and a computer set. The guide mentioned that every android should have this to be able to learn, so she took care of it.

"That's where you will live," she said. Raul looked around for a moment. "Do you like it?"

"Curtains."

"What about the curtains? You don't like them?"

"Better... different."

"Like what?" Etta's amazement was immense.

"Like this," he pointed to his new pants. "That color."

Just arrived in the world, and he already knows his tastes! It was unbelievable.

"Do you prefer dark blue?"

"I think... they would be good. Nice."

"Okay, you'll get dark blue ones." Etta decided not to pursue the issue for now. "You can decorate this room as you like."

"Can I, Domina?" Raul tilted his head and looked at her in a way, which, as she had already learned, meant a question.

"Etta, not Domina. And of course you can. It's your room."

The android moved slowly, walking around the room and looking at everything. He devoted the most attention to the computer. It was evident that he had learned in the factory what the device was for as he turned it on and touched the keyboard, activating the network. He looked at the screen for a moment.

"Can you read?" Etta asked.

"No."

"So you will start learning tomorrow. Before leaving for work, I'll leave you the right program."

"Okay, Dom... Etta."

The girl looked at her watch. She hadn't even noticed when the time to rest arrived. She took a sandwich from the sterilizer, ate it, and went to take a shower.

For the first time since she started to live here, she locked the bathroom door from the inside. She wouldn't be able to explain logically why she was doing it—unless she was just intimidated by this android, so much like a living man. She had no idea how she would fall asleep knowing he was here in the next room...

No, not next room. Shortly after the light went off, she heard light footsteps and felt Raul lift her blanket to lie down next to her. At first she stiffened, but then relaxed. She was the Dominant and she made the decisions. One word would be enough... but she did not say it. She had long been suffering from night fears, waking up with a tightened throat and an overwhelming sense of loneliness. She was afraid to talk about it with her doctor, who would probably recommend the proper therapy and withdrew her temporarily from work. She did not want that. She purchased the Easyhal and Opti inhalers, available over the counter, and decided to brave through it. Perhaps Raul's presence in her bed would help. She cuddled shyly to the naked chest of the android. She didn't expect it would be such a pleasant feeling... but his body was firm and velvety to the touch, and it smelled of freshness. It certainly wasn't a human smell, but pleasant and soothing. Only a heartbeat couldn't be heard, no breath raised this beautifully arched torso. She had to admit that this was even better. The muscular arm embraced her gently and caringly. She didn't even know when she fell into a calm, restful sleep.

Yes, Raul had been helpful from the beginning. All the more so now. Thanks to his efforts, on the next day, the girl already felt good enough to get up from bed and take advantage of the free time to summarize her students' results and evaluate their homework.

"You should rest," Raul said with gentle reproach, but Etta only grinned at the words. She wasn't used to being sick and she wasn't going to spoil herself. Raul's care was a bit astonishing to her—it did not fit her image of the androids. Was it yet another proof of the existence of "inner life" in an artificially created being? The thought kept coming back stubbornly while she checked the children's work and wrote comments on them—she wasn't able to shake it off. Now she remembered all the minor events she had witnessed: her Companion lifting the child, who had fallen and hit her knee, helping her neighbor with carrying down some old furniture, letting a butterfly out of her apartment window... Especially this last gesture was weird.

"Raul, why did you let this butterfly out?" she asked suddenly. The android, measuring medicine for her, froze in mid-movement. She didn't have to remind him of the details of the event, because the artificial brain didn't forget what had once happened and unlike the human one, it didn't distort the memories.

"A living entity," he said finally. "Our flat is not an ecosystem for butterflies."

"Great, but why did you care?"

That was a much more difficult question. Such behavior seemed quite natural to Raul, but what was the reason for this conviction? He obviously did not know. He stood motionless like a statue, with a dropper in his fingers, his eyes open and expressionless. He was silent, so similar to a doll in that moment, that in the end Etta got scared. His brain was given a problem to solve and was working on it, trying to find a satisfactory answer, and this could prove to be dangerous.

The young woman remembered very well the factory technician warning her, "Just be careful with abstract questions. Having stumbled upon an unsolvable problem, the android can 'freeze', not unlike a simple computer. In extreme cases, the problem is not reparable, because you know that this isn't a computer after all, and we can't just reset the whole system or defragment the main drive. A permanent freeze is basically the death of an android."

"Raul, come on! Forget about it!" Etta cried out, jerking up off the chair. To her immense relief, the android blinked abruptly, a sign of returning to an active state, combined with the rejection of the task received.

"Answer unknown," he said in a flat voice. "No data."

He finished the action he had begun, poured the measured drops into a glass of water, and handed it to Etta. She drank the resulting mixture, exhaling deeply with relief. Apparently, Raul himself didn't know why he was acting in that way, and not in another. Perhaps that was how it was supposed to be.

After the first week, Etta knew that her previous ideas about androids were wrong. Ordering a Companion was not the same thing as buying a computer or any other home appliance. Raul was not an obedient slave or an interactive toy. It was impossible to predict his behavior. Initially, he mostly sat at the computer, absorbing knowledge from the programs for androids. However, on the first full day, after returning home from work, she found the flat meticulously cleaned and all the dishes in the kitchen were ordered according to some mathematical scheme. The following few days were to reveal Raul's strange mania, moving the furniture in the apartment, rearranging the trinkets, and moving things so that they would be symmetrical versus some reference point. She didn't interfere with his actions—she was never too attached to the particular look of her apartment and she couldn't maintain order. In this respect, the android was a real help to her, although even she couldn't understand one thing.

How did Raul know what to do to make her happy?

She remembered that terrible day when she had to go to court to attend the case of the small, weeping girl. Brenda was only eight years old and was unaware of the crux of her crime, but she had to be punished according to the juvenile code—for putting her friend's health and life in danger. Because of her teasing, Julie Resnick was lying in the hospital, and doctors described her condition as serious. Etta was really horrified by what had happened, but at the same time, seeing Brenda and her parents, her heart filled with compassion. She remembered very well her practice in a juvenile jail for kids under the age of twelve. It was an extremely depressing place where children lost their childhood. She knew that none of them left the jail the way they came in, and it was not about understanding their mistakes at all.

On that day, when she returned home, she was mentally exhausted and cried as soon as she closed the door behind her. Until now, she was choking back her emotions—after all she couldn't show them, she was a teacher and thus was required to control her nerves.

"What happened?" Raul asked, rising from his computer. She couldn't answer him because sobs choked her throat and she shivered, as if feverish. The android came up and embraced her caringly. She clung to his chest, flooding it with tears. He stroked her hair in silence, since he couldn't comfort anyone and didn't have human empathy. He waited for his Dominant to explain to him what had happened and what the reason was for her strange reaction, but she didn't know how to tell him what had thrown her off balance. She already knew enough about androids to not to expect the impossible, such as compassion. Raul wouldn't be able to understand why Etta reacted like this to the reasonable consequences of someone else's actions, which, on top of that, had nothing to do with her.

"Just hold me," she whispered when she finally managed to use her voice.

"Do you want me to help you?" he asked.

"How?"

"You need to release this tension. It's bad for you."

She raised her face to him in surprise, and then he kissed her suddenly. He did it differently than a man, but still the touch of his lips, velvet and warm, was soothing to her. What was next? In fact, she couldn't fully understand how it happened that after a while they were both in bed, but it turned out to be a good solution. She stopped thinking about the court, about the two girls, each of whom was aggrieved in her own way, and the whole rigid system that required of every citizen absolute obedience to the rules. Suddenly it was only her and Raul, her Companion, her lover, that counted. It was probably on this day that she understood he really wasn't just a thing, but a being equal to people. If only others could understand...

III

Etta wasn't overly surprised when a week later, Veronica announced her intent to visit. She was only a little surprised that she asked Raul not to leave this time.

"What can she mean, what do you think?" Etta asked her Companion.

"It's hard to say when we don't know the facts," he said. "I will stay, if Miss Hornet wishes so."

She wished so, but why? Would it have something to do with the subject that she didn't want to talk about during her last visit? Etta was very curious about this secret, so big and important that Veronica had to keep a lid on it. And what did her remark about humanity being in serious trouble mean?

"Because it is," her friend said as they sat down at the table to eat and chat. "The ecosystem's resurgence is staggering, the seas probably can't be revived at all, and that's not all. Surely you have heard that in the past, Earth was the object of an asteroid attack. And what had happened in the past can happen in the future. Our scientists have already identified eleven large objects whose flight path may intersect Earth's orbit in the near future. It could have catastrophic effects. There wasn't much we could do about it before, but now we have an opportunity. We won't save the Earth, but we can save mankind."

"How?" Etta asked with astonishment.

Veronica looked around and then took a small device from her purse and set it on the table. After she switched it on, it began to emit a barely audible buzz.

"No one is going to watch us or eavesdrop on us now," she said. "What I want to tell you is strictly confidential. Well, a plan of migration of humanity toward the stars has been developed. For now, to Enceladus, where the first extraterrestrial colony is to be set up. Or rather, it has already been created."

Etta opened her mouth in surprise.

"Enceladus?" she asked after a moment. "But it's such a tiny speck. And there is no suitable atmosphere... no protective layer..."

"There wasn't. The work has been going on for two hundred years. Both have been created. Don't even ask about the cost."

"All right, but what does that have to do with me? What's the use of a colonist who can't have children?"

Veronica smiled. "Honey, people just like us are now of great value," she said with emphasis. "As the so-called administration for the colony. People on whom everything will depend. If the administration can't have their own children, it rules out the possibility of favoring them, as well as the danger of blackmailing high-level personnel with the abduction or murder of their children. Until the colony establishes itself as a stable society, people like us will be the governing class. The survival of the colonists will depend on us."

It took some time before Etta digested that message. So far, she had considered something like extraterrestrial settlements as a literary device only found in books and films, same as other people of her time period and past epochs did. It never occurred to her that someone was working on this seriously. And not just anyone, but the global government.

"Does it make you happy?" she asked after a moment.

"You bet it does. I've heard enough from my parents about how I'm worth nothing because I'm a zero, and that I'm a zero indeed. My brother had everything and they just wanted to get rid of me from the house as soon as possible. I have the opportunity to show that I am worth something, too."

There was a bitterness in Veronica's voice. Etta knew exactly what she was talking about.

"All right. But what does this have to do with our Companions?" she asked softly.

Veronica looked at Rasmus, who was exchanging some information with Raul. Fair-haired, skinny, with disquieting yellow eyes and irregular features, he had a too-big nose, awkward movements, and reminded Etta of something artificially created more than any other android. Ironically, he was more human than the others. Miss Hornet, a professional biocybernetician in government service, not only liked him but she also respected him, which he appreciated, showing her his affection in a touching way.

"Well, if we fly, they'll have to decide if they're flying with us," she said. "I don't want Brent to be treated like hand luggage. He will have to make the decision himself. I trust that you, too, will leave it for Raul to decide freely."

"But of course. I wouldn't be able to force him to anything. He is neither a thing nor my slave. He's... he's just my Companion. He has his rights."

"If only everyone thought this way."

Etta remembered the card she had found and the incident in the park and told Veronica about it. She listened grimly, nodding her head.

"This is getting more and more frequent" she said finally. "Such leaflets are recently tossed to all Dominants. I also received several, though I have not been thrown stones at yet. Be careful, no one knows how the situation will develop."

"Do you think it can get worse?"

"I do not know. Listen, Etta... think about what I said to you. Remember that you will have to leave behind everything you know. You have forty-eight hours to think about this. Then you must make a statement in writing about the decision you have made."

"I understand."

"See you in forty-eight hours, then."

After Veronica left, Etta wasn't able to calm down for a long time and finally decided to take a short walk. She needed that. She changed and went to the public space. Residential areas had been separated a long time ago from leisure and entertainment zone, where parks, cafes, amusement parks, and museums were located. The streets where houses were built were only used as residential areas, and for buying the most necessary of items in the stores located on the ground floor of each block. Everything was supervised by the police day and night. Wandering between buildings wasn't tolerated and such an approach reduced crime, such as robbery and home burglary.

Etta liked the entertainment area in the Milflores district. It was beautifully laid out and had all the amenities—a videoplastic park, a promenade, an entertainment center, numerous cafes and restaurants, dance floors, gyms, and even two casinos. The young teacher usually visited the park and one of the cafes, Rigores Plaza, which served delicious chocolate ice cream with an exceptionally tasty substitute of whipped cream. The recipe for this dessert was a company secret. In the past when natural ingredients reached absurdly high prices, the production of artificial flavors had become the most profitable industry. Large food chains had their own suppliers, and the flavors created exclusively for them were protected by dozens of patents.

At this time of day, Rigores Plaza was almost empty. Etta sat down at her favorite table, in the corner by the window, and ordered the Chef's Ice Dessert—a tasty composition of cream, chocolate and lecithin ice cream. The thought that there was not even a gram of natural ingredients in this mixture did not spoil her appetite. For a long time, natural foods were available only for the richest, except for the slim contingents, and everyone became accustomed to it. The synthetic ice cream was delicious and had the advantage of not threatening the health or the waistline.

Etta was halfway through her portion when an attractive blonde woman in a blue suit entered the cafeteria.

"Estrella!" she called. "How are you?!"

The teacher barely recognized her and almost choked on ice cream. "Sol! Is it really you?"

Sol Tarantino was her friend in elementary school. Once upon a time, they even made a childish blood pact, and then Estrella's mother banned her from watching television for a week, furious because of a bloodied dress... and even more for the hurt finger. Then they lost sight of each other, and now Sol was standing before her, smiling, with her hair dyed blond and the face clearly corrected by a skillful surgeon.

"Sit down, what's going on with you?"

"I finished my writing course and got a job at a literature factory," Sol said, nodding at the waitress. "For me, exotic sorbet with lemon liqueur."

"In a literature factory?" Etta wrinkled her nose. "I saw such an enterprise once. A huge hall and hundreds of computers... But it must be terribly boring!"

"Are you kidding?" Her friend looked at her with a pity. "It's a great job! You just get a topic and you have to elaborate on it in a set amount of pages. I specialize in serial crime novels. Last month, I was even sent for an internship at a police station so that I could watch how real detectives work. And a year ago, I was sent to a course on elegance and style to be able to describe the higher spheres more realistically."

"Well, I prefer what I do."

Sol put a spoonful of sorbet into her mouth and relished the taste with her eyes closed.

"And what do you do?" she asked after a moment. "I remember you wanted to be a teacher."

"And I became one. But before that, I graduated in history."

"Are you teaching in a college?"

"No, I teach lower elementary classes."

"Really? I admire you willing to spend energy on that. I hate children. That's why I stay away from marriage. I would have to get pregnant right away and give birth... what slavery."

Sol had a "two" qualification, but even as a girl she used to say with complete certainty that she would never be a mother. She couldn't stand crying babies or the babbling of older children, fleeing at their sight. She could never be persuaded to hold a baby when they had a compulsory visit to the nursery as their class fieldtrip, as part of their preparation for life in society. The teachers worried about her attitude, sent her to psychological counseling and therapy, and her parents worked on her all day, every day, but nothing helped. To their grief, a note was placed in their daughter's records: "Not suitable for raising children because of unstable mental structure." Thus, despite her genetic qualification, she could forget about a childbearing license, which she was happy with anyway.

"And I would love to have my own," Etta sighed. "Except that, unlike you, I will never have a chance for that."

"You should be happy. You can live as you want and do what you want."

"Unfortunately, not everything."

"Well, yes, it depends what you like. Are you lonely?"

"Not quite. I bought myself an android."

Sol's eyes became completely round. "An android? An artificial lover? Seriously?"

"What lover...? He is just a Companion, to have someone I can talk to after work. You might as well call him a substitute for a brother. Don't laugh!"

It was too late. Sol literally burst out laughing, until a few guests in the cafe started to look at their table with surprise.

"Please, Etta, you're going to push me into the grave," she finally said, wiping her eyes. "An artificial cohabitant... a battery-operated Romeo. I heard about such a perversion, but it seemed unthinkable to me. So how is he in bed, tell me?!"

"Oh, leave it," the irritated teacher pushed her empty ice cream bowl away. "You and your questions."

"Why leave it? It's a normal question. I know you've never had luck with guys, but I'd never thought you were so desperate. After all, there are dating centers, relaxation salons, why bring home such a thing?"

Etta took a big breath and counted to ten. Sol didn't understand anything, but it wasn't her fault. After all, someone who never had to deal with an android, as a rule, had wrong ideas about artificial intelligence. People saw only robots in the androids, only Dominants and cyberneticians knew they were beings, that they really thought independently and had their own personalities. In Sol's eyes, it probably looked as though her former friend had just confessed to a relationship with a vacuum cleaner.

"Let's just drop the subject," Etta said at last. "You probably can't complain about a lack of male companionship."

"I don't really care. I don't get involved in long-term relationships. I prefer a non-obligatory date, because when you're with a guy a little longer, he immediately starts to imagine that you belong to him and tries to dictate to you how to live. Sometimes I have the impression that men haven't changed since the caveman era."

Sol shrugged and ordered one more serving of sorbet, with an extra portion of whipped cream. She loved it.

"And how is your brother?" Etta asked. Brendan Tarantino suffered from tabes dorsalis and although the doctors were doing all they could, the disease was slowly destroying him. Even the most modern drugs were unable to completely stop its progression. Nobody knew why a young boy with a good genome had suddenly fallen ill with something extremely rare. According to medical records across the country, it was only the sixth such case in the last twenty years. It did not, however, change the fact that the therapy designed by the best physicians could only slow down the progression of the terrible disease that made Brendan more and more dependent on his family's help.

"Last year he asked for euthanasia," Sol said. "He didn't have the strength to fight anymore."

"Oh, I'm terribly sorry…"

"I'm not. Last year was a real tragedy for all of us. We took turns taking care of Brendan, so he wouldn't be left at the mercy of strangers, and it was awful. In the end, he had to have everything done for him, like a little baby… I know how it sounds, but I was glad he died before I started to hate him. He remained in my memory as a good and loving brother, not as a ball and chain."

Etta nodded understandingly. She had never been in such a situation, but she had heard about them. According to the common way of thinking, absorbing one's family with oneself was really in bad taste. Incurable patients who didn't want to undergo euthanasia moved voluntarily to state hospices, but they were a minority—people had long since ceased to fear death. They were much more afraid of losing their independence and of being unable to live on their own, and they didn't want to be a burden or a limitation on their family. They chose euthanasia, which allowed them to depart from this world painlessly and with dignity, and at the time of their own choosing.

"Anyway, I'm sorry," she said.

"In spite of appearances, I was, too, at least in the beginning," Sol confessed. "I really loved him. He was the only one who never called me ugly. Even my mom called me that. Compared to you, I looked like Cinderella. You know, maybe that's why I was so surprised that you bought an android. You have always been pretty; girls like you have no problems finding a boyfriend."

"Don't say that, honey! I never thought you were ugly, and besides, the most important thing is what one has in their head."

Sol snorted dismissively. "Crap! Say what you want, but everyone looks at your legs and face, not what you have in your head. I found out about that. As soon as I saved enough for plastic surgery and appeared at work with a new face, I started getting better jobs, and the boss decided to send me to the creative delegations. Before, I was sitting in the dark corner and writing articles for the last page of some shitty magazine. So don't tell me that beauty isn't important."

This conversation depressed Etta. As a primary school teacher, she had to teach children under the age of ten what really matters and how to assess the world. She was devoted to her work with all her heart and she believed in its importance. Sol made her realize that not everything she taught her pupils was quite true in real world, and it was an unpleasant fact. Repeating a hundred times that a person's inside is most important would not change the fact that beautiful people had it easier. After all, even the Companions were designed to please the aesthetic sense. Raul was beautiful—she'd ordered him like that. Nature made men fond of nice faces and shapely figures, and even if we didn't want it, our subconscious would propel us to favor those gifted with an eye-pleasing appearance.

No, not quite, she decided after a minute. *They say I'm pretty, but what does it matter, if genetically I'm just an irrelevant waste? He's the only one who doesn't care about it, only him... my Companion...*

She decided she would agree to her friend's offer. Since Earth couldn't offer her anything, it was better to leave everything and move to the unknown. With Raul.

*****

"...but these were all half measures," Etta said. "A truly effective fight for the environment began on the day of the adoption of Irwin's Law. This was the first so-restrictive law in the field of nature conservation, allowing for the execution of any poacher on the spot, and in addition to the traditional criminal liability, the confiscation of the goods of a person proven to be involved in trading protected species..."

This was her last lesson here. Looking at her class, she wondered if she wasn't acting crazy by accepting Veronica's proposal. She liked her job, she liked her stable life, and now she was about to throw it all away? But on the other hand, her friend offered her the opportunity to experience a wonderful adventure she hadn't even dreamt of. She couldn't give up this possibility, though it meant painful sacrifices. For example, she had to say goodbye to the school, and the children...

Easy, calm down, she reproached herself. *You would say goodbye to them anyway, next year at the latest, and the next class of five-and-six-year-olds would come in their place.* That's how it was when you worked at a school.

Despite the doubtless correctness of this reasoning, she felt sorry. She couldn't even say goodbye to her children as warmly as she would like—according to procedure, the children were supposed to think, like everyone else, that their teacher would only be leaving for a few days and then would return. A caution bordering on insanity, but it had its justification. In this way, all surprises and social unrest were avoided. The times of widespread access to information had been the times of chaos, and now that society had become an orderly structure, disturbances were treated as treason. Nobody wanted to return to old times. Mankind had received an overly painful lesson and, fortunately, learned to draw proper conclusions from it.

"Dear angels, I have to say goodbye to you now," Etta said, trying to make her tone as light as possible. "Circumstances have forced me to leave. I'm going to New Orleans, so I will not be here for a few days."

"Are you flying or going underground?" Jodie asked. "I would rather fly, you can look at forests and mountains.

"You can also fly and get killed," Esteban observed grimly.

"Esteban!" Etta tapped on the table. "Don't scare your classmates. Such accidents are very rare. No, dear, I'm going underground. It's a lot cheaper and I'm not making too much money... and I still have to pay the installments for Raul."

"So he will go with you?"

"Yes of course. He always accompanies me everywhere."

"And when will you be back?" Waylon asked miserably. He didn't take his round eyes off Etta, and she had the impression that he had a feeling something was up.

"I told you already, in a few days," she lied smoothly. "Mr. Yamato will sit in for me. You will definitely like him, he's such a nice young man."

"But it won't be you," Anissa said quietly. Her wide lips, always ready to laugh, curved down dangerously and Etta felt she herself would be crying any moment.

"You can't think that way!" she called out hastily, trying to hit a carefree tone. "If you don't get to know new people, you'll be bored! And now, so that you're not sad, we'll play the guesswork. What is all white, pink, and blue?"

It was only on the way home that the young teacher allowed herself for a few tears, although she wasn't really that sad. She knew she would miss her kids, it was inevitable, but the prospect of what awaited her was so colorful, so very appealing...

The other car passengers watched her with sympathy. Rarely anyone who was crying now in public, they guessed that something very bad must have happened. Except for one. When she got off, he came over and when she turned to see what he wanted from her, he hit her face with all her strength. Startled, she let go of the handrail and fell back to the pavement.

"Perverted fetishist."

Taking advantage of the stupefaction of other co-passengers, the aggressor jumped out of the vehicle and disappeared between buildings with the speed of lightning.

"Honey, are you all right?" an elderly lady helped Etta move off the sidewalk. "It's terrible. What did he want from you? You have to call the police."

"No, it's not worth it" the teacher rubbed her cheek red from a blow and checked her tongue to see if her teeth were in place. "I'm leaving soon, and the investigation would make it difficult for me. It's probably some mentally ill who has escaped from under the key."

"How is that? You won't report him? After all, this type can really hurt someone, they must catch him."

"Tell the police for me if you think it's necessary. They check the monitoring recordings and can easily track it down. I really have to go now."

"What did he call you?" the second passenger broke in, a young boy with a half-face face sprinkled with first beard. He frowned in disbelief, looking at Etta.

"Never mind" she forced a smile and shook hands with the elderly woman. "Thank you for your concern, but I'm really fine. I have to go, I have an appointment. Thank you again."

At home, Raul was waiting for her with two packed suitcases. According to the guidelines, they were supposed to bring only the most important things with them to avoid raising any suspicions. The rest was supposed to stay here, in their cozy apartment, as if they were going to return to it soon, although it was most probable that they would never return. Etta checked that all the systems were properly closed, except for the irrigation system for the window plants—it was supposed to work independently from everything—and then she went with Raul downstairs, where a slick limousine rented by a government center was already waiting for them.

Android studied her and finally touched the marks on her left cheek. She felt that a large bruise was forming there and she wondered casually how it would be explained to Veronica. She hoped that her friend would understand why she did not go to the police with it, although in this way she opposed the general law. The citizen was required to report this type of incident, and she neglected it.

For a moment, the young teacher felt her throat tightening, but after using the Opti inhaler, she managed to hold back her tears. Trying to look self-confident, she took a place next to Raul, who was calm as a rock. She noticed that the android was staring at her sideways and for a moment had the impression that he wanted to make a comment.

He did not say anything. Like most of the androids, he was more often silent than not, unless he had something specific to say. And since she said nothing herself, he guessed that she was not to be asked.

IV

The Personnel Selection Center was located outside the city, which in itself was a phenomenon on a world scale and testified to the seriousness of the whole undertaking. Unauthorized people not only couldn't enter there, no one even had the chance to find out about the existence of this institution, separated as it was from the whole civilized world. The resort itself was like a small town, equipped with gyms, a central clinic, and a scientific institute, to which Etta was invited after a thorough examination by a medical internist and a psychiatrist. Her S card wasn't respected here. All the tests had to be repeated, also endurance tests that she had never taken before. Only when a team of three doctors signed her fitness certificate could she rest in her assigned quarters. Raul had already prepared a bed for her, which she accepted with a grateful heart, as she was completely exhausted after that exciting day. She didn't even want to eat; she simply lay down and slept like a dog. The next day she took a shower, and after a good breakfast, decided to explore the area. Even though she had an appointment at the chief coordinator's office that day, it wasn't until the afternoon so there was no rush. She took Raul and left for a walk around the whole complex.

The resort was laid out nicely, and in its center there was even a small park with a pond, with floating water lilies. Etta was surprised to find that the pond was real, as were the floating plants and the grass that grew around it. Something like this was not seen every day, even in the richer neighborhoods. The parks there were designed and constructed by video artists. Beautiful, hygienic, and completely safe, they were a delight for the eyes of the walking citizens, but they were not real and everyone was aware of it. Here it was completely different.

There were several children of different ages playing by the water. Their sight reminded the young teacher of her class, so she turned away quickly and walked to a large automatic kiosk that looked like a vertical, flat display box divided into small windows. These compartments contained not only nicely wrapped cakes or drinks, there were also watches, small electronics, jewelry, and toys for children. On the side there was a press-o-mat panel with a newspaper selection keypad and a separate payment socket. Etta took the opportunity to buy the newest *Times*, and she was just finishing downloading the newspaper to her notebook when she heard desperate shouting from the direction of the pond. She hurriedly tugged the plug of the interface out of the socket and went back near the water, just in time to see Raul carrying ashore a shaken child, dripping with water.

"What happened?!" she cried out.

"He fell into the water," Raul explained to her. "He can't swim."

A young woman in an expensive, tailored outfit appeared out of nowhere and took the drenched child in her arms.

"I just turned around for a moment, I swear, and he disappeared!" she cried. "Timmy, my little treasure, how could you…? Oh, thank you, madam!"

"It wasn't me," protested Etta. "It was Raul who pulled your son out of the pond."

"But you told him to…"

"You are mistaken. I was at the newsstand. I didn't even know your child was in that pond. Raul himself made a decision how to act."

The young mother was still clutching at her child, who had already regained his courage and struggled to regain his freedom of movement. They were very similar to each other—blond hair, with some freckles and fine bones. Only the eyes of the woman were gray-green, not brown like the boy's. She glanced at the still android, her face showing a distinct consternation.

"Doesn't he have such cases in his program?" she asked.

"No. I see that you don't know the general theory of the androids and that you are dealing with a conscious being, not a complicated mechanism. Raul, tell me why you did what you did?"

"Danger of life, intervention necessary. Man can't live in water," the Companion responded with his gentle, softly modulated voice.

"This is a child. Do you know what a child is?" Etta continued.

"A child is a protohuman."

"A protohuman?"

"A human... who is... who is... small."

"Small, you mean short?"

"No. Small... not quite as it should be... ungrown. Undeveloped. Protohuman. Special protection. Have I done something wrong?"

"On the contrary. You behaved great, I just wanted to know why."

A long silence ensued. The android clearly looked for words that he could somehow match to the situation, but it turned out to be beyond his capabilities.

"I don't know," he said at last. "Because it was necessary?"

Etta looked at the woman, still cuddling the wet boy.

"Exactly. He himself isn't sure," she said. "Such things are not in any program. Make the boy change into dry clothes before he catches a cold. For Raul it doesn't matter, but for the small one, yes."

The woman reached out to her. "I am Oksana Nikolayevna Wysocka, a microbiologist," she said. "We have to meet again. Promise me we will."

"Of course," Etta assured her, hiding a bit of amusement. "Estrella Solis, a historian and the archivist of the expedition. I will be happy to meet you again, and also… Timmy?"

"His name is Timur. Timur Gongadze."

*****

All the same, Etta made sure Raul changed his clothes for dry ones. Although it was difficult to expect an android to get sick from the dunking, she felt strange when he walked beside her in wet clothing. Soon they had to part, as the time for the appointment with the chief migration coordinator, or rather a staff meeting, was coming, and it was pointed out that only people could attend it. Etta sent Raul to their quarters to change and wait for her, and went to the office center.

She was greeted in the conference room by a middle-aged man, fair-haired, except at the temples where the hair was slightly frosted. It was almost invisible, but a close look allowed her to see the gray. It seemed to be the result of some sort of life's worries, for his face was astonishingly young, with no wrinkles, and his intense blue eyes glittered with energy. His features were quite soft, without any stronger definition, but despite this, they didn't look effeminate—they were somehow masculine and decisive. When he was sitting, he seemed tall, but when he stood up to greet Etta, she noticed he was just of average height, not much taller than her. It was because he was well built, muscular and slim, although, as the girl assessed, he had a little too-short neck and a bit too-broad nape. However, it didn't ruin the overall positive impression, emphasized by a perfectly tailored military uniform.

"Hello, miss," he said cordially, clutching her small hand with his strong fingers. "Kirk Willner, captain of the expedition. Do I have pleasure of meeting our future archivist?"

"I think so," Etta said, somewhat abashed by such an exuberant greeting. "Yes, I am a statistician, archivist, and chronicler of the expedition, whatever that means. Are you... are you also the coordinator?"

"No, not at all. The coordinator will be here soon. Also a few others. There is a lot to discuss before the start."

"Before the start? Does that mean it's coming up soon?"

"Oh no, don't worry. There is still time, but please be prepared for many meetings like this one. Do you have an idea of the scale of the whole project?"

Etta nodded without a word. The longer she thought it over, the more she realized she was taking part in something unprecedented—in the abandonment of the mother planet by humanity. Not in the temporary resettlement, like for example, those who took part in the experimental lunar mining, but in an abandonment for good. On the other hand, the first colonists, who'd reached distant lands on wooden sailing ships, had to have similar feelings. They'd also abandoned their world and everything they knew for the unknown and never seen. Compared to them, today's colonists even had some comfort—they at least knew what the place they were heading to looked like.

In the meantime, others began to appear in the conference room—there were in total six men and five women, all with the badges describing their function in the future expedition. They looked nervous and intimidated, moved stiffly, and didn't know where to sit. Etta didn't know any of them; the recently met captain suddenly became the only person that wasn't quite a stranger to her in this great hall. Suddenly she regretted she didn't have Raul by her side.

When the hands of the old-fashioned clock showed three o'clock, the inner door slid open and a tall man with curly red hair, dressed in the official outfit—a white shirt with high collar, clasped under the neck by the metal logo of the institute for which he worked, and a black fitted suit made of matte fabric. He was followed by Veronica, equally stiff and official. She wore a similar uniform as Captain Willner, only better fitted to the figure—it was clearly a female version of it. Etta noticed just now the fabric from which both were made. It was bernit, the most durable "linen-like" material, as it was termed—flame-retardant fiber with thermoregulatory properties, capable of rapidly changing its molecular structure with the application of kinetic force. In a word, when absorbing the energy of the collision, it acted for a moment like a shield and could even stop modern bullets. She didn't know anything about its composition or production process—as the information was not publicly available—but she had seen the material before.

"I apologize for being late, I was summoned to the headquarters," said the chief coordinator. "Let's get started. My name is Kurt Nakamara. Most of you don't know me or anybody else here, but we have time to get to know each other. So far, there are thirteen of you, but there will be many more. All of us here belong to one group: the administrative department of the migration expedition. This is the first colonial expedition outside of Earth. Initially, as you know, the settlement was planned for the planet Mars, but the efforts to launch what was called a 'dormant ecosystem' turned out to be a catastrophe. The increase in atmospheric thickness, necessary for our purposes, resulted in an unexpected rise in surface temperature and the molten water from the poles created an environment that resembles a high-pressure steam bath. Despite repeated efforts, the situation was unstoppable. Meanwhile, Enceladus turned out to be a relatively easy object to work with. The automats working on its surface, without the need for any modification of their program, managed to saturate Enceladus's atmosphere with carbon dioxide and to sow terrestrial plants, which over the last century have raised the percentage of oxygen to the required twenty percent. The artificially produced ozone layer maintains radiation on the surface within the boundaries of what we have on Earth, and a high-orbit atomic stack provides the necessary energy and essentially replaces the sun. The research androids, sent with the last transport, collected for us data that confirms the successful completion of the work to prepare the colony. Remember that this is just a temporary colony! This is only the first step. Later, humanity will move to the stars, leaving its solar system forever."

Chief Nakamura paused dramatically before continuing, "We are the chosen people who will lead the colonists. The headquarters requires many things from us, but the most important thing is absolute composure and putting the good of the colony above one's own good in every situation. The psychological profile of each of you shows you have the necessary characteristics and therefore we will require it from you. Absolutely. The colonists will be like your children, depending on you and your decisions. You must not give in to emotions, not only from the moment of our launch, but starting today."

He paused again for a moment and looked at the gathered people.

"Most of you here have a zero classification," he said after a moment. "Many of you have Companions. Look at them and imitate their dispassion. Besides, your androids will also undergo specialized training so that they can be helpful in situations that threaten people. Miss Solis, your Companion saved a child from the pond, is that right?"

Etta stood up instinctively.

"Yes," she said. "Raul is very caring toward organic beings. I don't know if this is a feature shared by all the androids, or if he is somehow unique."

A short, restrained burst of laughter could be heard from the other end of the room.

"Please excuse me," said a thin man with short, dark gray hair. The suit hung loose and disorderly on him, although it was of good quality. His long, misanthropic face was covered with a two-day-old beard. It seemed as if he not only didn't fit his clothes, but anything in general, least of all this room.

"I am MacLean O'Leary, a specialist in inorganic reasoning and chief cybernetician of the expedition. Excuse me for interrupting, but... every android, every single one, is unique. There are no two equal among them, or even similar ones."

"Thank you for the lecture, Doctor, but we're not discussing the technical details now," the chief coordinator said reproachfully. "The creation of the Auxiliary Squad made of androids is one of the points in our plan, and therefore each of you who came here with a Companion needs to talk to him now about the resulting responsibility and the training that's awaiting them."

"Will they be taken away from us?" a petit woman sitting next to Etta asked sharply.

"No, of course not, Mrs. Wang. It is out of question. However, they will have separate training while you will be taking yours. I have gathered you here to make you aware of the most important aspect—that you are not participating in exercises or in games. You will really fly to another planet and you will have to deal with issues that our society doesn't have any clue of."

"How long will the flight take?" a blonde woman in a well-fitting outfit, sitting in the front row of chairs, asked.

"Four months, Mrs. Lavell. Because we will not fly in one ship, but rather in a convoy, we will not be able to accelerate faster."

"Why a convoy?"

"For at least two reasons. First, building a small fleet proved to be easier than building one big ship. Secondly, it is safer because in the event of a disaster, we might lose one ship and a part of the colonists, instead of everyone and everything."

"Four months… for a single ship, as I understand it, even shorter. It means that communication with Earth will be maintained, right?" Dr. O'Leary asked.

"Absolutely. The ship with the stocks we request, along with press and letters, will visit the colony at least once a year. Are there any more questions?"

"When are we flying?" asked someone in the back.

"Patience. The exact date will be given in due time. For now, everyone has to take the training described in the rules and regulations. My assistant will give you your assignments and I am asking you to make sure you meet the deadlines. You will be given the date of the next meeting in due course. For the moment, I thank you for coming and everyone is free for the evening. I advise you to make good use of this time because there won't be many such free afternoons."

V

Tell me…" Etta pulled Veronica's sleeve impatiently. "Why are you wearing a bernit uniform? What's up with this assistant thing?"

"Slow down!" Veronica ordered coffee and a pastry for each of them, and then she sat down. "I understand that you are surprised, but it must be like this for now. As far as everybody knows, I am an assistant and security guard for the chief coordinator. Nobody can know more than that, so don't betray me."

"Oh, you can be sure about that, we have known each other long enough… but what is it about?"

Veronica took a sip of coffee and looked around discreetly. The cafe was quite empty, and no one was looking at them.

"There is a faction opposing the expedition," she finally said quietly. "We are afraid of sabotage. Keep your eyes and ears open and if you notice anything, you can contact me any time, day or night."

"Is it so serious?"

"I don't know. We don't know much. Maybe all these precautions are exaggerated—and I hope it is so—but if not, then, you understand, we must be prepared."

"Why would anyone be opposed to the expedition?" she asked, fiddling with a spoon in her hand. Suddenly the cake lost its appeal to her.

Veronica bit her lower lip slightly.

"They believe it is unnecessarily exposing people. And that it is not going to work anyway, because the colony won't sustain itself and it will have to die. They also suspect some... government conspiracy."

Etta felt an unpleasant shiver. With current police methods, crimes were now rare, because they simply did not pay off for anybody. Nevertheless, they sometimes happened. And it wasn't just the illegal birth of a child or the unlawful entry into the green areas, or minor thefts or disputes... although the public media made every effort to make people believe that other crimes did not exist. But they were alive and well. They just weren't as publicized as they used to be.

"What do you think might happen?" she asked anxiously.

"I hope nothing. It is possible that this fear is excessive. But, you know..."

A tall man entered the cafe. Because of the dim light, it took a moment before Etta recognized him as Rasmus-Brent. He was in a uniform, similar to the one Veronica was wearing. He looked very dignified in it and very... human.

"I read once a very old book about an android whose biggest wish was to be like people," Etta thought, and then realized she had spoken it out aloud. She blushed. She was a little bit ashamed of her fondness of old books, of the yellowish-brown paper, sunken in the thin plastic, so much more cumbersome than tiny memory chips and universal readers. To think that people once only had paper books, their pages not even protected by plastic! It was unbelievable. How could people keep books with pages made of wood pulp, a perfect environment for the growth of bacteria, fungi, and mites, in their homes? People had no idea about hygiene in the old days.

"It's nonsense. Androids never want the impossible, it is against their logic." Veronica smiled at Rasmus. "What is it, Brent?"

"Good morning, Miss Solis. I'm sorry to disturb you, Veronica. I just want to say that you're needed to sign a training plan for the Asteroid team," Rasmus replied. "And Colonel Nakamara is waiting for you to report on the state of preparations for the implementation of subsection C of the preliminary schedule."

"Right. Tell the colonel I will be there in a moment." Veronica rose from her chair and put down her cup. "Forgive me, Etta. I have a headache to deal with."

"Sure, go. We will definitely find a moment for each other again."

Etta smiled reassuringly at her friend. After her departure, however, she saddened and rested her head on her hands. She never thought of criminals or crimes before. She grew up convinced that life was now safe and that policemen only had to show the way, to make sure that someone suddenly disturbed by emotions wouldn't hurt others, or to check on something that seemed unusual or disturbing to anyone. She knew they had considerable latitude in terms of checks and detentions, but after all, it had to be this way. As was said in school, the range of personal freedoms of every citizen was quite limited compared to what it was once, but it was due to this that mankind recovered from the monstrous catastrophe of the ecological collapse of the planet. And now she'd learned that crime as such still existed, only that information about it was blocked. There wasn't much information about the danger from space, either. What else weren't people told about?

Etta's thoughts were interrupted by a gentle tap on her arm. Raising her head, she saw Raul dressed in the same uniform as Rasmus had been wearing.

"The military patrol stopped me in the street, and they told me to wear this," the android said. "Why are there military patrols here?"

"Let me just say it must be this way," Etta sighed, standing up from the table. "I never thought myself I'd see a soldier up close, but it's the army that is organizing the migration, and the civilian scientific forces are under its control. Don't ask why, I don't know much myself yet. In any case, I'm not the only one waiting for training here. You will be training, too. You will become, I think, something of a rescuer."

Raul was silent for a moment, as always when he heard something unexpected.

"Does that mean I'll have to leave you?" he asked finally.

"Fortunately, no. I wouldn't allow that to happen, anyway."

Etta felt that if the facial expressions of the androids were better, she would see a sign of relief on Raul's face. She decided that at the nearest opportunity, she would ask Dr. O'Leary all about the psyche of the androids. She had no doubt that detailed research was being carried out on this subject, although the results were not generally available.

"Don't look for the soul in an android. They are just artificial creations, and the rest follows from the fact that we are all visual creatures. If their chemically assisted brains had a different package, you wouldn't have thought of treating them like humans," the headmaster of the school in which she worked told her once.

However, she herself could not resist the thought that Raul was not just a collection of complex circuitry and plastic fillers that pretended to be living tissues. No, there was more than that. According to her, he was a being, never mind that he was an artificially created one. A being. But to understand that, you had to live with an android day and night, watch him in daily activities, talk to him. Most people did not have the opportunity nor the desire to get to know androids. Apart from the cyberneticians, only the Dominants and doctors in the hospitals where medical androids worked, mostly as nurses, knew a bit more about the androids. The rest of society had no idea what the artificial Companions of men were, and their Dominants were often treated with indulgent irony. Just unhappy frustrates, who, like a lonely child, had to have a doll because no one alive would want to do be with them.

In a few decades, that way of thinking will change, Etta consoled herself. She really believed it. After all, the history of androids as Companions was very short. The first fully independent android was built only fifty years ago, and it had been only for the past two decades that they could be ordered… like custom-made shoes. That was when the production licenses were obtained by the first factories, able to conjure up a dream partner for anyone who had money for it. Big money, but possible to come up with, even in the form of a bank loan. Since the adoption of the relevant law, people with a zero classification even had a serious discount, subsidized from the state budget, since with the Companions, suicides due to loneliness had become rarer.

"No," she whispered. "If they were to take you away, I would fight to the death. I will never agree to that. Never."

*****

During the following days, there was no time for a social life. All the available time was filled with training and simulator exercises, with short breaks for meals. In the evenings, Etta fell exhausted on her bed and immediately fell deeply asleep. Raul took off her shoes and covered her with a blanket, then lay down on his bed and turned off his awake status for two to three hours, which was necessary for the battery that was his heart to switch on the energy regeneration circuitry. Such a system not only allowed the android to stay in good shape, but also complemented the illusion of his humanity, imitating ordinary human sleep. Now Raul needed more energy than ever, since the training of the support team, as his group had been called, was really intense. Of course, it wasn't meant to make the muscles stronger, because the physical parameters of the androids were factory-defined and impossible to change, but in other respects, the training program for the "artificials" was not so different from the "human" one. Androids had to learn the right reactions to specific situations, and there were thousands of situations, each more complicated than the next. Dr. O'Leary kept giving the Companions new challenges. In their electronic-chemical brains, the number of connections between memory blocks increased, as the molecules of the active gel—the composition of which was the manufacturer's strict secret—clung to each other, creating artificial dendrites and synapses, improving the exchange of information between the various sections of the blocks. This enabled the Companions to react faster and more precisely, analyze immediately, and create a program of action so fast that no human could keep up with them.

"Aren't you afraid that one beautiful day, these robots of yours will revolt against us?" Taira, the doctor's wife, in whom artificial minds awakened an atavistic fear, once asked.

"That is not possible," O'Leary replied. "They are not capable of the feelings that people inherited from their animal ancestors: a desire for domination or mere envy. And the Karpinsky Principle works here. They know that they were called into existence for the purpose of companionship. Not to help. Not because people weren't able to do some task. So they don't have a logical reason to try some kind of coup. Imagine another situation—people are building defensive androids that would fight for them. It is clear that they would begin to dictate to people how to live, because they are supposed to defend them, and the unmanaged man gets into trouble. The same applies to other key areas. No, Taira, we have designed for them such a role that they can't dominate us."

"Are you sure?"

"Positive. Karpinsky predicted everything. The general directive is that a person may ask an android for possible options of the action, but is himself responsible for the choice or for opting for yet another route. Man is the decision maker. Not android."

"I don't understand." Taira was an artist, she didn't understand anything about her husband's work.

"It's so simple, woman," O'Leary said, irritated. "Every android has a simple conviction engrained that people can handle themselves and they don't need an android's help. And in that case, the decision to take over leadership simply can't be born, because there is no support for it in the simple logic of circuits."

He waved his hand, and not for the first time thought he got married too hastily. His wife didn't fit in with him and they had too little in common. That's probably why she had left in the end...

Currently, Dr. O'Leary trained a support team at the facility whose existence was kept secret from almost the whole world. His wife had disappeared from his life a few months before, leaving a sarcastic letter that a man so devoted to his work should rather marry an android. That was why the doctor volunteered to take part in the expedition. Nothing held him back on Earth, not even in his hometown of Chichén Itzá. The government had offered him the opportunity to make a unique experiment, checking the suitability of the androids in conditions different from Earth, different than the greenhouse-like towns, in short, under combat conditions. MacLean O'Leary was truly passionate about his work, and he hadn't hesitated in agreeing to this proposal. Taira was a bit right. Her husband loved the subject of his research; it occupied the most important place in his life and he probably would be more disturbed with the destruction of an android than with the death of a man. And yet, the research objects treated him with reservation. They didn't trust him. If the androids felt something like trust, they denied it to the man who'd sacrificed most of his life to them. He clearly wasn't an authority figure to them, which they emphasized in a peculiar manner—they asked their Dominants, or Raul, who was appointed as the head of the team, for confirmation of his orders. It was annoying, but the doctor ignored the matter. He knew he wouldn't win with them, instead he would only become a laughing stock in the eyes of the people who treated artificials like ordinary machines. Anyway, it wasn't that terrible, since the androids learned new skills and in principle fulfilled the commands. And that was the goal, after all.

The human also went through rigorous training in order to learn how to deal with any situation. Some of the exercises took place in the field, which for most of the crew was a complete novelty. Except for two or three of them, none of them had set foot in an undeveloped area before and now they were taken to forested mountains with no products of civilization. People, accustomed to the pristine sidewalks of big cities, for the first time had the opportunity to stumble over the roots of a tree and the unevenness of the mountainous terrain with which they were told to struggle. The head coach did not forgive anyone and, according to a common opinion, she had a heart of stone. She wasn't moved by asking, moaning, crying, or even fainting—everybody had to do the exercises and pass the fitness tests, even if they had to take them several times. In addition, they had to listen to dozens of lectures and pass the exam for each discussed topic.

The trainings and lectures ended when colonists began arriving at the center. Initially, there were only crewmembers and administrators as the whole human foundation of the expedition. Now, those who were supposed to be its proper subjects started to appear. Men, women, children—all healthy, carefully selected and extremely excited about the upcoming adventure. There wasn't a single Companion among them. Families didn't need them. These people had each other, unlike Etta or Veronica, who were doomed to sterility. Both of them had their hands full now, anyway. They welcomed the new arrivals with a professional smile, provided them with the information they requested if it was available, saw that they were properly accommodated, and received everything they were entitled to. Etta rebelled against such a role, the role of a hostess, but Veronica accepted the things more stoically.

"We have to keep an eye on everything," she said, "to see everything and know everything, but in such a way that no one would suspect us."

"Oh, what did you get me involved in... but honestly now?" Etta asked directly. "I was supposed to be the chronicler and the statistician for the expedition, not an investigative agent. I feel like a character from a bad crime novel."

"There is no reason to. What is happening is a very serious matter, and the two of us are part of the security force for the expedition. Just like the entire administrative department, and even the scientific section. Understand, Etta, we have been involved in something absolutely unprecedented. We are in the army now—and it must be like this for society's good. Don't complain."

Etta did not complain, but she was tired of watching happy families. Seeing them made her painfully aware of how lonely she was and how much she was harmed by the current social system. Her friend didn't care about all that, but Etta just wanted to have her own family—a husband and children. And it was an unrealizable dream. If she had at least been a "one", there would be sure someone who would marry her. The "zero" man and the "one" woman, the zero-one relation—called "binary"—did happen and made sense. The law allowed for artificial insemination in such a case, meaning there was a chance for a child. But what man would want to waste his life with a zero?

Etta's bitter musing was eased by Raul, friendly and devoted as always. By his own will, not asked by his Domina, he began to stay with her on duty at the reception desk, filling out the registration documents. He did it much faster and more accurately than any man, and one could be assured that he wouldn't commit any typical human error in this work. This was an invaluable help for the girl, because she could focus on other things… and there were a lot of them. First of all, she had to tell the colonists exactly what was allowed and what wasn't, to check whether they had weapons, illegal chemicals, or unauthorized electronics, and to answer countless questions. Especially the latter was something that made her head spin, her legs tremble, and her voice to finally fail her. Etta was saved a little by the fact that she loved children—they were the ones to ask most of the questions—but Veronica sometimes had the impression that she was going crazy at the end of the day. Fortunately, the number of colonists was limited, just two hundred and forty families, and finally the blessed day came when the influx of people began to decline. Only the late ones kept arriving at the registration point when unexpectedly, the Cantoralles arrived…

VI

Estrella! How come you are here?! I would never have expected…" Nayeli Solis de Cantoralle stared at her older sister, unsure if she should be happy or to consider this encounter as some kind of a problem. Etta also asked herself the same, looking at Nayeli. The last time she saw her sister was when Nayeli was ten, but she recognized her immediately. Like all the Solises, she had these distinctive, luminous eyes with a black border and a narrow, aristocratic nose, but her hair was dark brown with a reddish shine, and her face was as round as a full moon. In general, Nayeli was rather plump and her figure got even worse after giving birth to two strong and healthy children, who were now hugging her, looking curiously at their aunt, whom they saw for the first time in their lives. The boy could be six years old, the girl certainly not more than four. They were both as dark as the Indians, but their eyes were gray, after their mother.

"I'm working here," Etta said after she had gathered her thoughts. "And how come you are here?"

"We've signed up for the program," a cheerful voice said from the corridor. "Hi, little one."

A tall, handsome man with dark skin, blue-black hair, and dashing, shiny black eyes appeared in the office.

"Hello, Dario," Etta said dryly.

"What's with this reservation? There was a time when you greeted me much more effervescently!" Dario laughed freely. "Is that how you welcome your own sister and your favorite brother-in-law?"

Etta muttered something, and Dario turned to the children, "Itati, Amador, what's up with you, why are you standing like that? Say hello to your aunt!"

"Good morning, Auntie," the children said almost simultaneously, although without leaving their mother's side. Their gaze expressed a certain distrust. They had probably never heard of Aunt Estrella, and it was hardly surprising. Nobody brags about the fact that they have a zero in the family.

"Good morning," Etta replied, deciding to get a grip and not to show her discomfort. "You will now come into the scanning chamber, one by one. In the meantime, Raul will take care of your documentation."

Dario looked at the still android, and a mocking smile crept across his mouth.

"You have an artificial secretary here? Does it use lots of oil?"

"Raul is not a secretary and he doesn't need any oil... unlike some people," Etta said through her teeth and walked over to the desk with the monitor. "Enter the chamber, Dario."

"Whatever you say, sister-in-law."

Raul raised his head from the stack of flat pods. He took one of them and activated the "write" option, as he had done hundreds of times. He didn't seem to even notice the young man's remarks.

"Please come here, ma'am," he said to Nayeli. "Sit down and put both hands on the table."

Nayeli took a chair with dignity and began to respond to the standard questions, while sensors embedded in the table recorded her physiological readings, sweat composition, and fingerprints. The times when only basic fingerprints were recorded were gone. Meanwhile, Amador, taking advantage of the lack of adults' attention, looked curiously at the whole room, then circled the desk, stopped, and suddenly kicked Raul in the leg. The android looked at him without emotion, while Etta, who saw the whole scene through the corner of her eye, shouted sharply:

"What are you doing? Stop it immediately!"

"But he doesn't feel anything," Amador protested. "He's like a chair."

"A chair?! Get away from Raul, now! And before that, apologize to him."

"I need to apologize to an artificial? Dad says it's just a machine…"

Etta stopped the scanner and turned toward him. She was really angry and it had to be written on her face, because Nayeli paled at her sight.

"Come here to mommy, honey!" her sister called hastily.

"Listen to me, young man," Etta said menacingly, staring at her unruly nephew with a blazing gaze. "Take note that the androids are neither things nor machines. I don't care what your ignorant father or others like him say about it. Raul is a living being and you have to respect him, is that clear?!"

Amador contorted his dark face in a grimace of sudden terror and burst out weeping. Little Itati joined him in solidarity, although she probably didn't understand much of what was going on. Nayeli jumped up and embraced the children.

"You see what you've done?" she cried angrily.

"What's going on?" Dario's alarmed voice came from the scanning chamber. Also Veronica, attracted by the screams, looked into the office.

"Any trouble?" she asked.

"No," Etta said. "Would you kindly take over these visitors? I've had enough of them. Raul, we're going to our quarters."

"I have just a bit left," the android objected.

"Doesn't matter. Rasmus will finish for you, we're leaving."

Veronica looked at her friend, then at the unknown woman, pale with anger and hugging the crying children, and nodded.

"Go, we'll finish here for you," she said. "We'll see each other tonight; we'll talk then. Brent, take over the interview."

Raul gave Rasmus the pod with its writing lights flashing.

"I'm sorry for this confusion around myself," he said to Nayeli, who didn't even look at him. "It was nothing important."

And he followed his Domina. Etta walked in huge strides, not looking back until she reached her quarters. Only there did her rage leave her. Sorrow took the best of her and the girl cried, sitting on the bed. Raul, as usual delicate and discreet, sat down silently beside her, embraced her, and waited for the attack to pass. Fortunately, Etta was able to get over such moments quickly, and soon she was able to get hold of herself, although she allowed Raul to hug her and stroke her head with that steady, soothing movement. The awareness of his strength and absolute devotion was necessary to her, and she couldn't quite understand how she could have managed without her Companion until recently. Finally calm, she pulled out of his embrace and stood up. Initially, she had intended to explain her reaction to him, but she gave up on the idea. It was enough that she would have to explain the whole situation to Veronica. The android wouldn't understand some aspects of it anyway.

She went to the bathroom to wash her swollen face with cold water and brush her hair a bit. She had a great desire to take off her bernit uniform and take a long shower, but she decided to postpone that pleasure till the evening. For now, she still had to bring reports to the chief coordinator's office, pick up some documents, and check whether the decision to include her in the military finally arrived. She didn't want it—but Captain Willner convinced her it would be better for her. As a soldier, she would have wider authority both during the expedition and later, when it would come to the management of the colony. Veronica had also made a request to be included in the military, but she had done it much earlier, and had already received her assignment and was studying for the officers' exam.

The chief coordinator accepted the documents she brought, signed them in right place, and asked about the mood among the colonists. He seemed to be a little worried.

"Ultimately, we have to have about five hundred children here," he said. "Most of the colonists are families with many children. We made sure that the age range is as narrow as possible, so that once we reach the colony we will be able to organize something like a school. But for now, you understand that we have to be very careful about these kids. You know kids. What can we do so that they don't get bored and get into too much trouble?"

"I can gather volunteers and organize day care," Etta suggested. "Those, whose parents will be in training, will be supervised and entertained there. Colonel... can I ask you about something?"

"Sure."

"On what basis did the recruitment take place? After all, it wasn't through an official announcement that colonists were sought for an extraterrestrial facility."

The coordinator smiled understandingly.

"Well, not quite. In fact, we have dissipated the news about looking for families with children to settle in a specially adapted island in the Pacific Ocean. As you probably know, the government has been trying to reactivate the ecosystem on the islands for decades, unfortunately without results so far. This is the irony of history, but it was easier for us to remotely adapt Enceladus than to repair what our thoughtless ancestors destroyed. Earth is dying. Our efforts only slow down its agony."

"Now I understand," Etta whispered and added. "And the flight? I understand that once they are in the center, people can no longer leave, and I also understand that this is the reason for so many troops here. But the flight will last, as you said, for four months. Don't you expect the possibility of rebellion in space?"

"Of course we do. Anyway, it's not only the looming rebellion that constitutes a problem, but also the flight itself. That is why we decided that all colonists would be put into a medical coma and placed in water tanks for the purpose of shock absorbance. We need to reach the top acceleration possible, and only the control rooms will be equipped with g-force leveling. If we wanted to do it for the entire ship, every ship, we wouldn't leave before the end of the next century... the costs, you understand."

"I understand. So the control personnel won't go to sleep?"

"Definitely not all of them. If you agree to go with me for dinner, I'll explain everything to you. In a nutshell, the ship's automatics will be supervised by the androids, but because this could cause Karpinsky's Paradox, they will be watched by people. Taking turns, of course."

"Karpinsky's Paradox?"

"Yes. Ask Dr. O'Leary, he'll explain everything to you. Oh, and congratulations. From now on, until you pass the officers' exam, you will be listed as a Cadet Solis. And please remember my invitation."

Etta instinctively stretched and saluted. The coordinator saluted her back with a smile and the girl left his office. She wasn't sure yet if she would agree to go for dinner with the coordinator, but she wanted to. She had grown to like this eternally busy man with red hair, twisted like shavings, and eyes green as lettuce. He wasn't very handsome, but after getting to know him better, everyone was fascinated by his magnetic personality, and above all, his extraordinary intelligence. He was totally devoted to his work, so much that it seemed that he didn't think of anything else, so his invitation surprised Etta. Did he like her? True, he was always nice to her and he treated her very kindly, but something more?

It was still early, so she decided to visit the inorganic intellect specialist right away and ask him what that paradox was about. What was Karpinsky's Paradox? Henry Karpinsky, she knew—he was the creator of the general theory of androids. He'd formulated the principles, according to which a basic program had been developed and applied to the "newly born" brains of androids of both sexes. However, that was where her theoretical information ended. The rest she knew from her own observation, or guessed from Raul's behavior. She definitely needed a conversation with a specialist.

*****

The insistent call to the door was effective, but only after a few minutes had passed. Finally the door opened a little, and in the resulting gap Etta saw the figure of the Irish doctor. He was wearing dirty pajamas, his face was unshaven, and his breath— she felt it even from the distance—smelled of cheap whiskey. He wasn't surprised to see Etta.

"Please come in," he said indifferently. "Don't mind the mess."

It would be difficult not to mind. The doctor's room looked like one big trash bin that matched the neglected look of its resident. The doctor scratched his ribs and hesitantly waved his hand for a moment, pointing somewhere between the chair and the couch.

"Please sit down," he murmured at last. "Would you like something to drink?"

"No, but you will have something to drink. Coffee," Etta said decisively and headed for the kitchen. She managed somehow to find a clean pitcher, two cups, and brewed strong coffee without sugar, adding only the synthetic chocolate which she always had herself. The doctor grimaced but drank obediently. He seemed to be resigned and despite a large dose of alcohol, deprived of any will.

"You are just like my wife. She also put chocolate in her coffee. And she also didn't like when I wanted a drink after work," he said grimly.

"It's not my business how you spend your free time, but now I would like to talk to you," Etta said. "And besides, don't you care about your health?"

"It's not your health, so leave it to me." O'Leary helped himself to more coffee. His hazy eyes cleared a little. "So what is it you need from me? Does your Companion complain about my teaching methods?"

"Not at all. But I have a request for you. I want to be your student."

"Excuse me?"

"I want to study, learn. I want to be an android expert."

"It won't be easy because you will have to start practically from scratch…" O'Leary looked at Etta with more interest than before and with some new respect.

The girl nodded. "Yes, I know. My knowledge is practically nonexistent. For example, what is Karpinsky's Paradox?"

"Oh, that is a very simple concept. The point is that in some cases an android, who is supposed to take care of the well-being of a man, can consider that killing him without asking him for an opinion would be the best option for that man. It will be logically flawless even though contradictory to the assumptions."

He was still looking at Etta. His blue, seemingly faded eyes were the only bright spot in a tired face scattered with stubble.

"Why do you want to study andropology?" he asked suddenly.

Etta stiffened and looked away.

"I want to search for the souls of the androids," she finally said reluctantly. Dr. O'Leary looked puzzled, but it was expressed only by a slight smile. He finished his coffee, put down the cup, and stood up.

"Well, in that case, you have plenty of work ahead of you," he said. "Even me, although I know every single detail of the construction of the androids, the smallest nuances of the chemical composition of the materials used, and all the programming options... well, I wouldn't be able to derive a mathematically accurate proof that an android has a soul."

"But you know he's a being, not a machine."

"You know, I rather believe in that more than being a hundred percent sure. It is not as simple as it seems. When dealing with a self-organizing program, at some point it is difficult to answer the question of where all possible options provided by the constructors end, and the spontaneous invention begins."

"Why?"

"Because we lose count, and in the end we don't really know whether if what is there is the result of what we have introduced, or not. Androids are quite different from each other, but it's not proof of anything yet. Well, if you want to..."

The doctor went to the bookcase and opened the decorative door. He chose one of the tiny boxes of data carriers resting inside, and handed it over to the girl.

"This is the basic textbook," he explained. "Get acquainted with it thoroughly. Then I'll ask you about it and give you the next one. The media is compatible with most modern optical players."

Etta put the textbook carefully into the compartment on her military belt. Actually, she didn't like having to wear a uniform at first, but with time she had to admit that it was a very functional outfit. She didn't even have to carry a purse because all the useful little things fit comfortably in the waist compartments, and she gained full freedom of movement.

"See you then, Doctor," she said with a sigh. It was strange, but she wanted to stay there in the apartment that looked like a battlefield, and talk to an unshaven misanthrope in dirty pajamas. *It didn't make any sense,* she thought.

VII

When she reached the cafe, Veronica was already waiting for her. She was sipping a fruit smoothie and thinking about something, staring at the setting sun. The bernit uniform fit her as well as her favorite secondskin clothes, and the two men talking by the next table looked at her with obvious pleasure. Veronica paid no attention to them.

"Sit down," she said at the sight of her friend. "Tell me what happened at check-in. I already know that the woman, Nayeli, is your sister, but you probably didn't get upset just because of that."

Etta sat down and ordered vanilla cream for herself. Sweets always improved her mood. They spoiled her figure, though, so she usually avoided them.

"Yes, she is my sister," she said grimly. "My sister, my brother-in-law, and their children. And my bad luck that they applied for the program."

"So you don't like them much?"

"It's not the point. You see, Dario Cantoralle practically grew up with us. He is the son of our neighbors. They used to leave him with my parents all the time. As you may have noticed, he is a typical lady-killer, and when I was a teenager, I was hopelessly in love with him. I visited my family quite often then, though I had lived with my aunt since I was twelve to be closer to school... and in reality, because my family was ashamed of me. I couldn't help but stare at Dario. He knew it well, the trickster he was, and used me to cover his mischief. You can imagine how I felt about his marriage to Nayeli, even though I was an adult already and I lived and worked in Caracas."

"Is he a two?"

"No. He is unlimited, imagine that... I didn't have a chance. Nayeli is a three plus. All our family has good qualifications... I am the only one who is a zero. I tried to forget about them all and live as if they never existed. I almost succeeded in that. And now, they come here out of blue, and their son dares to kick my Raul!"

She spoke the last words with such ferocity that her friend couldn't contain laughter.

"I'm sorry," she said after a moment. "But the child isn't guilty, you know that."

"I know, of course I know! It is Dario who brought him up this way. I don't expect wisdom from Nayeli. She has always been stupid, so I'm sure it's Dario who educates the younger generation of Cantoralles. He belonged to the Peoplists organization as a teenager and, apparently, he still holds on to those ideas."

At the mention of the Peoplists, Veronica frowned slightly. She didn't like the organization and was afraid of its actions, because they called for the complete exclusion of the androids from social life. Their motto was "People for People" and their dogma claimed that androids disturb social integration and are a very harmful prosthesis of ordinary social relations. The rap sheet of the organization included a number of incidents of attacks on factories in which androids were assembled, as well as on "finished products".

"It's been a long time, maybe he's grown up?" Veronica suggested timidly.

"Somehow I don't believe it."

She stopped because Oksana Wysocka came over to their table with a tall, gray-haired man with a bit of a wild look. He had a heavily curved nose, brown eyes, an abundant mustache, and sharp features, like the native Indians. His appearance brought to mind a hazy picture of mountains, sharp wind, and horse riding.

"Let me introduce you... this is Tengiz, Timmy's father," Oksana said. "He just got here. Important affairs kept him in the city."

"Lieutenant Colonel Tengiz Gongadze, the chief surgeon of the expedition," the man introduced himself, saluting to the girls, who immediately sprang to their feet. "At ease, I'm here unofficially."

He took a seat at the table and ordered drinks for all without asking for preferences. It was evident that he had been used to ordering people around for a long time. As he said himself, he was a doctor, but his behavior was that of a professional soldier from the old days.

"Oksana told me that your android saved our son," he said to Etta.

"Raul... he just reacted to the threat," the girl replied. "He always does that."

"That's peculiar, you know? Most of the androids, if they are not given a command, will not take any action even if someone hangs himself near them." Gongadze raised his glass. "*Salut.*"

The girls drank obediently, assessing that the drink with a name unknown to them contained a bit more alcohol than they were used to. Veronica, who had a very sublime taste, realized at once that it was composed of grenadine, cream, coconut milk, tonic, and very strong and very sweet banana liqueur. She decided that the mixture was very tasty, though it should be enjoyed in moderation.

"I don't know too many androids besides Raul," Etta said carefully. "It is hard for me to say whether he is objectively superior, or just smarter."

"Intelligence has nothing to do with it. You know that Brent has an IQ of 240, and I don't think he would try to save the boy," her friend interrupted. "He'd most likely start to give him instructions on how to swim, because he would find it more logical."

Tengiz Gongadze smiled, showing his teeth, sharp as an animal's.

"Logic aside, I know that androids act sometimes in surprising ways," he said. "Fortunately, they are not troublemakers, and as you can see, they can be helpful. I am grateful to Raul for what he did, though I think that Brent's system would not be bad, either."

"Tengiz!" Oksana cried out reproachfully.

"What? You spoil the boy too much, I told you as much long ago. He doesn't even know how to swim yet, as you can see. Time for me to take care of him."

"There you go. That's why I didn't want to stay with you. One day Timmy will decide for himself if he wants to be a soldier like you, but I will not allow for him to be brought up as a soldier."

Seeing that the conversation was taking a dangerous turn, Etta interrupted it by asking, "So the entire medical division reports to you?"

"Yes, Miss Solis," the lieutenant colonel answered, "but as a member of the command section, I will fly on Alpha ship. The remaining doctors and nurses will be separated so that no ship is without medical care. You know, just in case."

"I understand, of course. And you know, my whole life I had no idea that the military still existed at all. I thought it was formed just for show, only in its name similar to what it used to be."

Gongadze smiled indulgently and with a bit of superiority.

"We need people to think so," he explained. "But as you see yourself, a permanent army is indispensable, even today. Well, the rules have changed a bit, but not that much. We are here to enable the civilians to live and to develop civilization in peace. Otherwise, peace, culture, and mutual friendships would make them so bored that they would eventually slaughter each other to the last person."

Veronica laughed at this unceremonious vision. Her pale cheeks were slightly pinker from the alcohol she had drunk, and mischievous sparks danced in her eyes.

"Well, we are already in the army," she said, sipping the last drops from the glass.

"I know. We're striving to make the whole migration service militarized. For safety and efficiency. Not everyone likes it, but that's the way it is."

The lieutenant colonel gave her a glance with obvious pleasure. He liked her, and it wasn't surprising—he was not the only one in the resort to notice how pretty and attractive this girl was.

"Do you know when we're taking off?" Etta asked, playing with her glass mechanically.

"Don't be so impatient. Enjoy the last days on Earth instead, since you will probably never see it again."

"We are still waiting for the chief chemist. She is supposed to arrive this week, and then the staff will be complete," Oksana said. "We're finishing up the medical testing of the colonists. I suspect that we will get the order to leave before the end of this month."

All the candidates to be colonists had to pass not only the qualifying tests for the migration program, but also a very meticulous testing in the center itself. Biochemical exams, various types of fitness tests, those for intelligence and those checking various fields of knowledge—there was plenty of it. Then there were also mandatory training sessions and practical exercises, most of them so that the colonists wouldn't roam unnecessarily around the center and stick their noses into matters that they shouldn't have too good of an idea about.

"I wonder what's awaiting us at Enceladus," whispered Etta.

"There is a well-equipped colony waiting for us," Lieutenant Colonel Tengiz laughed benevolently. "The views will be a bit unusual, it's true, but everybody will slowly get used to it. The first few days might be difficult... when we wake up the colonists and they find out they are not on Earth, it will be hell."

"Couldn't you announce that openly?"

"Are you kidding? If the news spread that we're sending people, especially children, to another planet, we wouldn't be allowed to take off. We can't be sure that something hasn't been leaked anyway... opposing organizations could already plan some sabotage."

"Tengiz, don't be so paranoid."

"I have to, it's my job."

To be honest, Etta didn't really believe in the possibility of someone sabotaging the mission. She had heard about it a couple of times already, as both Veronica and Captain Willner had mentioned it, but for the young historian, who grew up in a quiet city, it was just unthinkable. Perhaps the unincorporated—that is those, who fled to the outskirts of cities to live without supervision and machines at every corner, without mandatory tests, without vaccines, without Easyhal and Opti inhalants... in a word, to live as people did ONCE—but not normal people! And yet, in light of what she found out here, at the resort, the unincorporated people were not a threat. These romantic "flower children" did harm to nobody but themselves, because wasn't it a harm to voluntary renounce civilization and the safety it created? No, they weren't aggressive. True subversives hid within the integrated society, camouflaged so well that all kind of precautions had to be taken while organizing the migration.

Etta liked Tengiz Gongadze, although she would have sworn earlier that she didn't like men like him. Even just that he was a soldier... Since childhood, she had heard that they were like a separate nation, people to be avoided, but which had to exist to maintain social order. They were compared to sewerage systems—they were necessary for hygiene and health, but no one should approach them except from the relevant services. So it was also with the military and the police. They were tools: dirty, blunt and repulsive, but necessary, so they were tolerated. Meanwhile, at the Personnel Selection Center, Etta had met soldiers and found out that they were completely normal people, no worse than others. They were neither killing machines nor beasts without feelings. They had their own world, their own purpose in life, their own social structure, and even their own culture. It had to be like this. By joining the army, they renounced their nationality, because from that point on, they belonged only to the armed forces of the planet Earth. Tengiz Gongadze was one of them; he even got his medical degree at the Military Academy. He was a soldier in his soul and his heart, it was obvious from the first glance. He had a posture of a warrior, springy moves of a cat, and the gaze of a man accustomed to issuing orders. She thought, however, that she understood Oksana, because she also wouldn't like to live with such a man.

"So you are separated?" she asked. "And Timmy... how does he take it?"

"Very well," Oksana said. "He knows that some parents live with each other and others don't, and that it has nothing to do with their feelings for their children. Because of him, we stay friends and never argue."

"Well, otherwise, the kid would be taken away from you," Veronica said maliciously. "The Educational Services Department has no sense of humor."

"That, too," Gongadze admitted reluctantly. "We had to be very careful, and before we could be put on the list, we had been instructed to live and act like a normal married couple here, meaning in the colony. We both, as well as Timmy, were signed up on this condition."

"And where is he now?"

"He's sleeping. Corporal Svensen stayed with him. She loves children a lot."

"Corporal Svensen? Which one is she?" Veronica drew her eyebrows together and searched her memory for a moment. Finally, she shrugged her shoulders with resignation. She didn't know all the soldiers yet.

"She is a young soldier," Gongadze smiled under his mustache. "She's in the security department assigned to the staff. She's a milksop when it comes to ordinary life issues, but she knows how to fight, she can take orders and the kid is safe with her."

"An armed woman…?"

"Woman soldiers can be more dangerous than men. Women in general are able to be ruthless and fearless. Well, but not necessarily Svensen. She would be better off on the front line than at a social gathering. Suddenly she turns out to be timid, scared, and hiding in a corner like a twelve-year-old at an adults' party."

He laughed cheerfully, revealing his strong, yellowish teeth.

"How many children will be in the colony?" Oksana asked.

"Nearly five hundred," Etta said. "I was discussing this with Coordinator Nakamara. They specifically selected families with three or four children, or as a last resort, two with prospects for more. Timmy will have company."

"Including your niece and nephew. What are they like?"

"Actually, I don't know them. I saw them for the first time in my life when they came to the office, and this incident with Raul spoiled everything."

It wasn't easy to keep a secret at the center, so everyone already knew about the incident in the office. Some were surprised by Etta's nervous reaction and reproached her for arguing with her family "for no good reason", while others— those who had their own Companions—supported her firmly.

There were also those who tried to mediate, but they didn't achieve anything.

"Have you tried to reconcile with your sister somehow?"

"With Nayeli? It's hopeless. When I was sent to my aunt, she was only ten years old, but already by that time she considered me a stain on the family honor. Actually, my parents sent me to Aunt Paulina because of her and Johnny, my older brother. They couldn't stand me."

Gongadze grunted sympathetically.

"Yeah. A zero in the family is often treated like a fifth wheel in a car. You are not the only one with this problem. I have encountered soldiers of both sexes in my practice who enlisted only to have a pretext to escape from their loved ones. In the army it doesn't matter. It's even desirable."

Etta smiled slightly and shook her head.

"Something like this never occurred to me. Forgive me, Doctor, but I was taught that the military is not something appropriate for the people of my social class. Don't get upset, now I know it's not so, but it is hard to get rid of the mental habits infused since childhood."

"I understand. It is normal for the public to distance themselves from uniformed formations and think of themselves as something better. But it is us who maintain the society in balance."

"I don't deny it."

"Come on, Tengiz, let's talk about something else," Oksana interrupted. "When you begin to praise the army, you bore your audience to death. Miss Solis, please tell us something more about that android of yours. What is it about him that you are defending him so strongly?"

Etta opened her mouth, then closed it, finally reached for her glass to take a drink.

"I can't explain it," she said, embarrassed. "You have to live with the android to understand what kind of being it is."

"Isn't it the same as sexine, only more advanced?"

"Not at all, Mrs. Oksana. Believe me, an Android Companion is not a lesser being than a human, and better than many of them. However, I won't give you further explanations because it is impossible to do."

"Speaking of the devil…"

Raul approached the table, greeted everyone, and then turned to Etta. "Sorry for disturbing you. Coordinator Nakamara wants to see you. It's about the school programs. The proposals just arrived and he doesn't know which package to choose."

"What school programs?" Veronica was interested. Etta stood up hastily.

"The colony education programs for the children," she explained. "It's very important. Excuse me."

To be honest, she was glad she had an excuse to end the conversation. Although she knew more about androids now than the average person, she still had no idea how to talk about them to people who were strangers to that topic.

VIII

Etta was slowly walking back from the meeting. It was a warm evening in late June, the first stars appearing in the sky, and the young woman wondered, for the first time since she arrived here, if she was sure she wanted to leave Earth. Even so ruined, it was still beautiful, and what could be waiting on far-away Enceladus? On the other hand, it was necessary. The small satellite with the artificially created ecosystem was to become the first extraterrestrial colony. The children who grow up there will go to the stars, leave the solar system forever, colonize a planet they have never seen before, and have their own offspring there. Mankind will survive even if the Earth is destroyed. This thought was kind of reassuring, even joyful in a sense, in spite of the awareness of the huge risks involved. Work on the Expedition 1A—as it was codenamed—was supposed to last twenty years. During that time, the children on Enceladus would grow up, practice the needed skills, and absorb the necessary knowledge.

"And what if they encounter aliens?" Etta remembered the Oksana Wysocka's naïve question and laughed quietly. It had been proven that there was no intelligent life within the distance reachable by human-designed vehicles, so there was no such danger. Research also yielded other results. For instance, the improved spectral analysis allowed scientists to establish beyond any doubt that life evolving on Earth-like planets could not be significantly different from the ones on Earth. The same amino acids that made up the DNA of terrestrial creatures, and similar atomic configurations, were found everywhere.

"Life on Earth is what it is, not because of a chance, but because something different would not have the chance to survive and evolve," Professor Haskiel said. "We can safely assume that if there are conditions similar to Earth on other planets, then the life there also will be of the terrestrial type. I don't mean the evolution of humanoids here, though it can't be ruled out. Human construction is, on the one hand, universally functional, and on the other hand, has enough shortcomings for the need to develop the ability to compensate for them, and thus to think creatively. Reason doesn't come out of nowhere, my dear. It is an evolutionary necessity, and with lack of such necessity, it simply will not develop."

The professor spoke much longer, justifying the optimism of the forecasters in all possible ways so that in the end, there was no time to discuss the results of the training so far. The remaining points of the meeting were postponed for the next evening and people were dismissed to go to their quarters. They were already very tired… after all, they had been running from one meeting to another since morning. Only little Timmy's father seemed to have bottomless energy. Timmy's father… Etta still couldn't find a neater description for Tengiz. He wasn't Oksana's husband, although they had a child together, and tact didn't allow the former teacher for more detailed questioning of the Russian woman. Both of them loved little Timur, though they had completely different vision of what was best for him. The boy did not suffer any harm from this difference of opinion, however. He was a trusting, outgoing child and, as it seemed, he loved both parents equally.

Etta stopped by the house, enjoying the scent of the wild violets and sweet pea that had been sowed on all the green islets, leaned against one of the young trees, and closed her eyes.

"Waiting for someone?" An unexpected voice snatched her from her thoughts. Next to her stood Dario. She hadn't even heard him walk over. He stood two steps away from her, handsome and masculine, as self-confident as ever since she got to know him.

"No, I'm walking back to my quarters," she said harshly, unhappy that she let herself be surprised like that. "And you? What are you doing here at this hour? Shouldn't you be with your family?"

Dario shrugged. "Nayeli is putting the kids to sleep, and it's gonna take time. They always want her to read to them and argue about which fairy tale to choose," he said. "I preferred to go for a walk. Do you live alone?"

"How is that your business?"

"I don't know. I thought you might have someone."

He smiled, flashing his white teeth. He knew well that she still liked him and like any man aware of his good looks, he didn't even consider a different possibility.

"No, I don't. What do you want?" Etta asked reluctantly. He didn't seem to be offended.

"Well, why don't you invite me in then," he suggested. "You know I always liked you. If you hadn't been a zero, I would have definitely married you, not Nayeli. Don't misunderstand me, I really like her, but she's a silly goose and for sure she's not as pretty as you are."

"Dario!"

"What? Don't pretend to be a prude. What harm would there be if we cuddle together a little bit?"

Etta turned indignantly toward the house, but her brother-in-law grabbed her by the shoulders and turned her face toward his again. He was much taller and stronger, too strong for her to break free.

"Get off me, you bastard, or I'll start screaming!" she yelled.

"As if you didn't like it. I'm better than your overgrown vibrator that you pretend is a man." Dario laughed and tried to kiss her. Etta twisted desperately, trying to push him away, when suddenly a great force tore her brother-in-law away and lifted him in the air.

The girl jumped back, catching her breath. Raul was standing in front of her, holding a struggling man by his shirt. Etta could swear that she saw a brand new, unfamiliar expression in his slightly clenched lips.

"Leave me alone, you crazy vacuum cleaner!" Dario rattled. "You'll crush my ribs."

"Put him down," Etta ordered, regaining her calmness. "Nothing happened."

Raul followed her order without a word, but didn't step back. He was still standing between Etta and her unlucky, furious wooer. Some undetermined threat was lurking in the motionless figure of the android. The young teacher had never seen him like this before.

"I'll make a complaint and you'll be scrapped, you, you…" the fuming Dario stopped, apparently searching for a word strong enough.

"Just open your mouth, and I'll complain about you," Etta shot back. "Get out of here immediately, and don't you dare come closer to me, because you'll regret it. It is only because of Nayeli that I won't ask for your immediate removal from the center."

Her brother-in-law mumbled something insulting through his teeth and disappeared into the dense darkness. Only then did Raul look at Etta.

"Did he do anything to you?" he asked with obvious concern. Etta shook her head.

"No. Thanks to you."

She stroked Raul on the shoulder, sensing the tone of the artificial muscles under the smooth fabric. She wanted to ask him something, but she changed her mind. He wouldn't give her a sensible answer anyway. It would be better to wait until tomorrow and ask that question to the expert.

*****

She couldn't sleep despite the extra dose of Easyhal. In the early morning hours, she managed to get a short nap, but at dawn she was already on her feet. She took a hot shower, dressed in her uniform, and went to the cafeteria where she expected to find Dr. O'Leary. There were four such facilities at the center, plus two large restaurants. Most of the colonists and almost the whole crew ate their meals there, not willing to bother with cooking, and their accommodations weren't equipped with food vending machines. MacLean O'Leary usually ate breakfast in the Little Black cafe, and lunch and dinner, if he had the time, at the Hazel restaurant. Both of these premises were close to his quarters, so he didn't have to walk far. Sometimes he appeared in his pajama pants and an undershirt, but after a brief initial surprise everyone became used to it. Someone who knew him from Chichén Itzá spread the gossip that the doctor was a known eccentric and he never bothered with what people thought of him, especially since he was irreplaceable in his work—well, that explained everything.

That morning, O'Leary was sitting at one of the tables in Little Black, eating pancakes and drinking white coffee. At the sight of Etta, his skinny face, bleak as usual, brightened a bit.

"Please sit down," he said, pointing at the chair in front of him. "Have you read the textbook yet?"

"Well, I'm still in the first quarter. It is a very difficult book and I don't want to just skim it." Etta sat down and ordered a lemonade. "Doctor, I have to talk to you. You are the person responsible for the androids, not just the expert on their construction and behavior, but also a sort of the coordinator, right?"

"True. So what's the problem?"

"I have to tell you something. Raul attacked my brother-in-law yesterday."

O'Leary became serious. "Why?" he asked, putting the fork down.

"Dario was insistent toward me," Etta said. "I might in the end have managed to push him away on my own, but Raul intervened. He didn't hurt him, but he treated him a little bit roughly. He seemed kind of strange to me... jealous? Is it possible?"

The Irishman sighed and rubbed his temples with his fingers.

"Theoretically, no," he replied after a moment. "They don't feel typical human emotions. But we can't be sure about it. I will say it in another way—the scientific opinion on this issue differs from the conventional wisdom. As I have explained you already, we don't know exactly how the brain of a single android works. Contrary to popular belief, they have their equivalents of feelings, so jealousy could have existed, or something very similar to it. However, in my opinion, a completely different mechanism was at action. Possessiveness, caused by fear of loss. You can't even suspect how difficult it is for an android to face something like a loss of their Dominant. The reaction to this can be severe, even a permanent freeze."

"I haven't thought about it before."

"The technology to produce Companions is relatively new, not even a single generation has passed since the introduction of the program. There hasn't been much comparative material yet."

Etta tried to imagine what an android would feel when he suddenly lost the purpose of his existence, but her imagination failed her. After all, she didn't even know how androids felt normally, whether they wondered about something like the purpose of existence, and whether they needed it.

"There are so many questions. Raul can't answer them for me, I have no idea why." She sighed finally.

"It's clear… what is it that you don't understand here? An average person can't accurately describe the processes that take place in his brain tissue either. It's absurd to think that Raul would know everything about his own construction and operation, just because he's an android. Be careful with such questions, because you may harm him. Please remember that a Companion is safe from everyone, because he doesn't have to answer any question if it is beyond his capabilities. He has the freedom to make decisions. But that doesn't apply to you."

"Why?"

O'Leary put a piece of pancake in his mouth and chewed it for a moment, pondering. Finally he swallowed and replied, "See, just because he WANTS to answer you. For you, he would be looking for answers until all his circuits freeze. You must be careful. And avoid your brother-in-law. It is better not to provoke situations like the one yesterday, because it can lead one day to disaster. Unfortunately, we don't live in a fairy tale, there are no "laws of robotics" like Asimov wrote about, and an android can kill a man if he considers it justified."

"I'll be careful," Etta promised him. "Thank you, Doctor."

"Please tell me whenever you have such problems."

Because of this conversation, she almost was late for her officers' exam. The examiners undoubtedly noticed her nervousness, especially Captain Willner, who immediately sent her a reassuring smile. She rarely saw this energetic, always cheerful man, but she realized that she liked him almost immediately after the first meeting. As Oksana explained to her, it was Kirk Willner's nature to win the sympathy of others. The woman knew him well, since he served in the same corps as the father of her son and sometimes visited her. Little Timmy loved him with his whole heart, and Etta had to admit that the captain was exceptionally warm and affectionate toward the children. Before one of the meetings, she even asked him why he spent time in the day care, where he came several times a week, especially given everything else he had to do.

"I love children," he explained seriously. "Unfortunately, I'm a 'strong zero'. Whichever way you look at it, I probably won't have my own children, blood of my own blood. You have no idea how it hurts."

"I do have an idea," she replied. "I'm a zero, too."

She expected something like "yes, but…" but the captain just embraced and kissed her—not insistently, but like a good friend. For a moment, hugged to his broad chest, she felt something strange. After a while, she defined it as a sense of total security, and an awareness of being extremely important to someone. She told Veronica about it.

"There's nothing strange about that," her friend replied. "He is the expedition's captain. He has been selected appropriately. He must inspire absolute trust, adoration, and respect at the same time. This is the basic requirement for the function."

Well, he inspired such feelings. He treated everybody with friendliness and respect, regardless of their position in the hierarchy. People felt good in his company, as if infected with his raw energy, humor, and self-confidence. Maybe that's why, seeing him in the examination committee, Etta felt relieved and even managed to smile. Soon enough, she also found out that the exam itself was not even half as scary as she had expected, though it went on for a long time and covered all the parts of the material from the evening courses.

After the session, it turned out that Veronica had organized a small party at the cafeteria in honor of her friend's promotion, which, as it turned out, happened on her twenty-fifth birthday. A cake, streamers, and alcoholic cocktails awaited the freshly minted lieutenant—the exam for university graduates allowed skipping of the NOC levels. Embarrassed, Etta was surprised to find that she was more popular at the center than she thought.

Her diligence, commitment, invention in organizing children's activities, and nice character won her a lot of sympathy, and the cafe was filled with what seemed like a whole crowd of friends congratulating her. For the first time since childhood, she felt surrounded by a family... even better, because her own family didn't treat her as well. After all the hugs and kisses, she finally sat down to catch her breath, and then one more pair of strong, though small hands embraced her neck from behind. She turned around, surprised.

"Esteban!" she cried out. "How come you are here?"

"I came with my mom," the boy explained to her and pulled on the hand of a woman next to him, his other hand in Etta's.

Etta had the opportunity to meet Hermione Ponce, the mother of one of her former students, for the first time, and she was amazed by her beauty. This woman looked like a Greek goddess—tall, with an impeccable shape and regular features, classic nostrils, and her fair hair combed into a stylish bun. Only her expression was hard, non-feminine, and her beautiful lips didn't smile—she had been through too much for it not to leave its mark on her.

"Hello. Mrs. Ponce," Etta said, offering a hand to her.

"Hello. Estebanito told me a lot about you, and I wanted very much to meet you," Dr. Ponce said, squeezing her hand. "I'm the head of the science department here, the chemical section."

"I'm very pleased. I'm happy Esteban is flying with us, he's such a good boy."

"I'm glad I could take him. Luckily, his father already has children with his second wife, so he doesn't need him." Hermione became even more sullen. Obviously she was still trying to deal with what had happened to her.

"I'm so glad you're with us," Etta said softly.

Hermione sat down beside her and sat the son in her lap. The boy hugged his mother, still not letting go of his favorite teacher's hand. Etta watched him with compassion. She had always treated him with greater understanding than the other pupils, knowing the tragedy he had survived as a six-year-old, barely three months after starting school.

"I am also glad that I got the chance to do something with my life," Dr. Ponce said. "And that I could take my son with me. What do you think, will this colony work?"

"Of course," Etta assured her with all the warmth she could give. "You will be a really important part of this colony, too. The chemical section is a strategically important point."

"You speak like a military tactician."

"Well, I'm now an officer, but don't mind it. I am the same as before, only in uniform."

"There are a lot of uniforms here. I didn't think that this project was managed by the military."

"It is better for everyone."

"It's hard to get used to it."

Esteban moved abruptly and asked, "Are there other children here?"

"Of course, a whole lot. You will see, you will have fun here," she promised him. "And now, tell me, do you want a piece of birthday cake?"

"Of course!" The boy became livelier at once. While putting his cake on a plate, Etta caught Veronica's meaningful glance. She knew it well—it meant Veronica had something important to tell her.

"Excuse me for a minute. Honey, here is your cake, and you can help yourself to anything else you want," she said, getting up. "I have to talk to somebody."

As soon as she approached Veronica, her friend pulled her toward the corner.

"The migration plan disappeared from the coordinator's office," she whispered. "As soon as you get back to your quarters, pull out all the data you are responsible for and encode it with key number four. Bring it to Nakamura in the morning."

"I can send it…"

"Better not. The connection can be hacked. Record the data on media and bring it with you. All of us have received a similar command."

"Fine. It won't take too long, I will do it as soon as I return to my quarters. I don't want to leave in the middle of my own party, especially when my favorite student is here…"

"It must end before the curfew anyway."

The center was under military control, and at ten o'clock in the evening all the lights had to be turned off. A night lamp was permissible when someone wanted to read, but not full lighting, not to mention a social gathering. Everyone was used to the curfew and twenty minutes before ten, the party dwindled by itself as the participants went hastily to their quarters. Etta also rushed to her place, leaving the cleaning to the waiter machines. In her room, she first closed the shutters to be in compliance with regulations, then sat down at the computer.

"You are not going to bed?" Raul asked.

"I have to work a little. I'll go to bed as soon as I'm done."

"You will not get enough sleep. People need around eight hours of inactivity per day to be fully functional."

Etta looked at her Companion with some surprise. This wasn't the first time he'd made similar comments. She knew androids were taught first aid and nursing on special courses, but she didn't think that Raul would behave like her personal doctor. She suddenly wanted to know if other Companions had also acquired such strange manners.

"People are very flexible," she said finally. "They can sometimes skip a big part of their rest period without harming themselves. And I have to make an important report for the coordinator tomorrow."

"I'll help you."

"You don't have to, it's a simple job. I'll be done in an hour. Take a shower and go to bed."

"Okay, but not now. I'll recharge the battery and then come."

Etta nodded approvingly. She knew what he meant. Each android had started a self-charging cell in a separate room so as not to expose people to radiation from the minicore. This meant that she would have enough time to compile the data for the coordinator, and maybe she could even manage to use the shower before Raul returned.

IX

No, it was not a delusion. Chief Migration Coordinator Colonel Kurt Nakamara was lying on the floor of his office, staring at the ceiling with his unseeing eyes. Beneath his back was a black pool, frozen in an irregular stain on the carpet. Etta staggered. A moment ago, she had wondered why the office was so cold. Now she was sweating, as if the furnace was suddenly set to at least one hundred degrees Fahrenheit. For the first time in her life, she saw someone dead. It took some time before the girl pulled herself together and went to touch the telecommunication button. She quickly selected the number of the expedition's captain. She didn't even think about calling anybody else.

Kirk Willner showed up in the office a few minutes later. He patted Etta on the back and immediately proceeded to examine the corpse, muttering something to himself. Finally he straightened up and looked again at the trembling girl.

"There is no doubt it's murder," he said. "I'll let the doctors know we need the results of the autopsy as soon as possible. We also have to check if anything disappeared, and if so, how, and what was it. Who knows best about the contents of this office?"

"Veronica, I think."

"Call her."

The serenity and self-confidence of the captain gave a bit of courage to the young teacher, although she still couldn't control the tremors in her knees. She obediently called Veronica to the office, while Willner spoke to the medical services. She noticed he was using a special encoded line.

"Do you suspect something or someone?" she asked when he finished.

"You know, somebody must be behind it. There is no way around it," the captain said dryly. "Such things don't happen by themselves. We still have to let Colonel Gongadze know... he will have his hands full. And we need to close the center. Nobody will get in or out of here until we clear up the matter."

Etta remembered what Veronica had said about the opponents of the expedition and again shivered involuntarily. Willner noticed this and placed his hands on her shoulders.

"Don't worry, we'll catch him," he said emphatically. "Use the Easyhal and stay here. We will need your testimony."

Etta nodded obediently, struggling to suppress the urge to hug the captain and seek solace in his strong arms. This would be exceptionally improper. She took the Easyhal inhaler from her belt pocket and took a strong breath. After a moment, the horror passed, only a cool thought and calmness remained. She stopped trembling.

Veronica appeared at the crime scene along with medical services. Certainly not as shocked as Etta, she still looked out of balance. She hardly noticed her friend, absently replied to Willner's greeting, and paled at the sight of the coordinator's body, even though she had been prepared for it.

"Register everything and take the body," she instructed the doctors, having recovered from the first shock. "Captain Willner, please arrange a cordon around the office. No one but me has the right to leave or enter until I have finished the inventory of everything that is here. We need to know if something has disappeared."

"Yes, ma'am," the captain responded, as if to someone with a much higher rank. At this point, Veronica was in charge of the operation, and he acknowledged this without any discussion.

The doctors finished the visual registration, then carefully transferred the body of the coordinator to the stretcher.

"One moment." Veronica stopped them. She stood over the stretcher and stared at it with a strange intensity. For a moment, she clearly tried to remember something, wrinkling her forehead and moving her lips silently.

"What is going on?" Captain Willner asked finally, worried by the prolonged silence.

"I don't know. Something is wrong but I can't figure out what... Okay, I'll think about that later. Take him. As soon as the autopsy report is ready, send it first to Dr. Gongadze and to me, and a copy to the chief commandment."

"Are we waiting for the report before notifying the staff?" the captain asked cautiously.

"No. I will send the initial report to General Lazinsky. And above all, we have to notify Lieutenant Gongadze. He is now the main decision maker here until new orders come."

"Not you?" the captain blurted out.

Veronica looked at him sharply, as an officer at a subordinate, and Etta realized something that she should have understood a long time ago—her friend had a much more important function in the chain of command than she had imagined. She remembered the old, now forgotten expression: gray eminence. It seemed very adequate here.

"Not me. My job involves different tasks. I can't sit at the desk."

Captain Willner nodded, waited for the surgeons carrying the stretcher to pass him, then walked over to Etta.

"Let's get out of here," he said softly. "The investigation is underway, let's not disturb it. They will call us if we are necessary."

The girl obediently stepped behind him, feeling that despite her Easyhal, her knees were still wobbly as if something had hit them. For a moment, she wondered whether she should take another dose, or one of Opti, but opted not to. She preferred not to risk losing her objectivity in such a tense situation, and mixing the two popular medications could bring her into a kind of mild euphoria—something very nice, but disrupting proper judgment.

Kirk Willner took Etta to a cafe by the command center, made her sit at one of the tables, and ordered a fortified coffee with real sugar.

"Drink it, you will feel better," he said affectionately. "Cognac would be even better, but in the situation of an internal alarm we have strict abstinence rules."

"I understand, Captain." Etta thought that especially today, she would have gladly had something stronger to drink. But if it's not allowed, then it is not allowed. She understood it perfectly, though despite the uniform and the training, she still didn't feel like a soldier.

The captain handed her the coffee and sat down opposite her.

"Let's call each other by our first names," he suggested. "I have a higher rank, but we are not in the British Royal Navy. All right, Estrella?"

"All right... Kirk," the girl replied, hesitating for a split second. Her innate shyness caught up to her again, although life in the center had dampened it slightly. But in front of such men as Captain Willner—handsome, strong and very masculine, every inch a warrior—she always felt intimidated. She felt much more comfortable among intellectuals.

"Do you know Veronica Hornet well?" the captain asked, sipping his coffee.

"We went to high school together. We were roommates for eight years—also at the university, although we studied in different faculties."

"In high school? Not too early for self-reliance?"

"Our families were eager to get rid of us by sending us to a boarding house in the capital. You sir... you didn't have such problems?"

"No. My parents loved me very much, kept me close, and had difficulty with 'cutting the umbilical cord' or whatever it is they say. I'm sorry you two had to manage on your own, it couldn't have been easy."

"Easy... no, that's true, but we had each other. We've been friends since the first meeting and almost inseparable for the next eight years. Actually, we are the only true family for each other."

"I see." The captain drank from his cup again, not taking his blue eyes off Etta. "But your sister, with her husband and children, arrived here recently, correct?"

The girl nodded reluctantly.

"Yes," she said. "But so what? I have never been friends with Nayeli, her children are afraid of me, and Dario... he better not come near me."

"They are afraid of you? Impossible. You get along with children perfectly well, they adore you."

"Well, yes... but not these two. I made a scene at the beginning, and now they both think I am a witch. I wonder myself why I exploded like that. After all, Amador's kick couldn't have hurt Raul."

It was true. The longer Etta thought about it, the less she understood her own behavior in the check-in office. Why had Amador's behavior upset her so much? In the end he was only a child, he didn't know everything, he didn't understand everything.

"Maybe because an android means more to you than to a lot of people," Willner said seriously. "To you, he is a man. You not only like Raul but you also respect him."

"And what are the androids to you, Kirk?"

The captain moved nervously and looked to the side. It was clear that this topic wasn't easy for him.

"I'd rather not answer that question," he muttered after a moment. "It brings back sad memories."

"I'm sorry, I didn't know."

"It isn't your fault. It was a long time ago, I was just an NCO then. My then-supervisor, Major Geoffrey Hunter, had a Companion, Rachel 82F…"

He paused for a moment. Etta covered his broad hand sympathetically with her delicate hand.

"If that hurts you, don't talk about it," she said softly.

"It's not pain, it's a deep shame. I have to live with it, although I would like to erase that event from memory. You see, I behaved like a terrible egoist. Major Hunter had a zero classification, though not as strong as mine, and so he decided to get a Companion. At first sight, Rachel was pretty ordinary, but she had a personality, and boy, what a personality it was. Because I was the major's orderly, I had a lot of contact with her, and I became somehow obsessed with her. As I now think about it, it seems to me that I fell in love with her, although I would not call it that then. The thought itself seemed absurd to me. But the desire to get Rachel for myself took the best of me, and for that reason I started to plot. I will not bore you with the details, I will only say that I persuaded my distant cousin, Doreen, who was a one plus, to start dating the major. Geoffrey fell in love with her, and seriously at that, so he decided to marry her. Together they could apply for a baby from artificial insemination. That was my goal. Married people don't need Companions, and I thought I could ask for Rachel for myself. Indeed, the major agreed to my suggestion with relief—he probably thought it would be best for everyone. I was crazily happy. I didn't take into account that she might also have feelings. I think it didn't seem possible to me."

"So what happened?"

"If only I knew… The thing is, I'm not sure. On the day of the wedding, Rachel left the house and never returned. No one knows what happened to her. The investigation found nothing, although it went on for a long time. I made sure it would."

"Do you have any suspicions?"

"Yes, and it kills me. I suspect in this way, Rachel expressed her protest against treating her like an object. I think she did an act of self-destruction, otherwise we would find something. Anything."

Etta kept her hand on his. She felt the captain had told her something he wouldn't confess to anyone else, and that he needed her touch very much now. He was not quite a man made of stone, though he sometimes pretended as such. As a commanding officer on this scale, he probably had to behave unfazed by everything, but—what Etta understood now—it didn't come easily to him.

"We all make mistakes," she said. "They are impossible to avoid."

She wanted to say something else, but at that moment the loudspeaker said: *"Attention. Captain Kirk Willner, please report to the command center. All colonists are asked to remain in their quarters until dismissed. A state of emergency has been implemented in the center."*

"Here it starts," the captain said, rising up hastily from the table.

He was right. From that moment, things moved very fast. Patrols were strengthened, meal delivery was organized, and two detectives from headquarters arrived—a civilian, Erik Karlson, and a military officer, Major John Carter. Both of them wanted to see the crime scene first, but Veronica didn't let them in until she was absolutely certain that only the staff list had disappeared from the office. It wasn't clear whether someone had taken it to mislead the investigation, or came for this document specifically and the coordinator surprised him. The internal monitoring system of the office had been deactivated very skillfully, not only so the records couldn't be read, but also the traces of manipulation were thoroughly obliterated. The external cameras also didn't record anything suspicious, but here the investigators managed to get some sort of a clue: a quarter before midnight there was a brief pause in the recording. It was a well-thought-out and well-executed action, as it was only discovered after a careful analysis of the time stamps on the record—at some point, the clock started to be a dozen seconds late. The investigators needed only to determine in which moment this delay began to learn the time when the murderer appeared in the office. Unfortunately, nothing else could be found in the initial stage of the investigation. The staff interviews didn't bring anything new, either. Detectives planned to interview all the colonists now, but as that was a job for several weeks, they decided to wait for the autopsy report first. It could reveal some details that would narrow the pool of potential suspects, and this would be very handy for them.

X

Oksana Wysocka arrived last to the meeting. Etta smiled in a greeting, but the microbiologist did not return her smile. On the contrary, she seemed to avoid her eyes. She looked frightened and embarrassed, and she was visibly upset, much more than it could be expected. Etta felt a pang of anxiety. What else could have happened?

"Ms. Wysocka will present us with the autopsy report," Erik Karlson said. "Oksana Nikolayevna, please."

Oksana took a seat on the dais and cleared her throat twice. It was clear that she didn't know how to start, but feeling the pressure of many eyes on herself, she finally started her report.

"As you know, I have the competency of a pathologist and I was therefore assigned to carry out the autopsy of the chief coordinator. Together with my team, we have conducted a thorough autopsy, trying not to miss anything. The official report will be available to all interested in the Mission Command Center, and I will present its key points here. Kurt Nakamara was undoubtedly murdered. The crime was most likely perpetrated by a single individual who came behind the coordinator and, after a brief fight, broke his neck with a karate blow. Mr. Nakamara collapsed on the broken drinking glass, thus his injured back and the blood on the carpet. The event took place between midnight and three in the morning. Determining the exact time is impossible, because the person that had been there set the thermostat to a temperature close to zero, and this caused the body to cool down. It is significant that even though the body had bruises, caused by compression, it evidently received a single blow. The assassin was well trained and precise. He knew what he was doing and under no circumstances was it a murder of affection or an accidental death as a result of an unplanned fight. We have collected all the microscopic trails we could find. After excluding those coming from the crime scene, only one clue remained, namely the presence of AN-type macromolecules on the coordinator's shirt, firmly embedded in the fiber structure.

Dr. O'Leary, sitting two chairs away from Erica, stiffened visibly and released the air between his teeth with a soft whistle.

"What does it mean?" Lieutenant Colonel Gongadze asked.

"Would you like to explain, Dr. O'Leary?" Oksana turned to the Irishman. He grimaced and bent his head as if someone hit him hard in the stomach.

"That means a struggle with an android," he said reluctantly. "And I know what you will say next, Oksana Wysocka! And I will say that I would advise extreme caution in formulating conclusions."

The silence was broken by excited voices all over the room.

"Quiet!" Detective Karlson yelled. "If anybody has something to say, ask for the right to speak!"

Physicist Tao K'ung raised his hand.

"Dr. O'Leary, is it possible for an android to commit murder without an order from his Dominant?" he asked, turning to MacLean. The Irishman shrugged his thin shoulders.

"If he considered this action logical, then yes," he said reluctantly. "An android is not a remote-controlled toy. Most people forget that they make independent decisions."

"So why do they obey their Dominants?"

"In professional jargon, this is referred to as the Jinn Syndrome. As we all know, the jinn from the fairy tales is unpredictable and arbitrary, but because of a sense of gratitude, he served the one who let him out of the bottle. Just like an android. Knowing that the Dominant is the cause of his creation, he feels obliged to him. That doesn't mean, however, that it cannot act on its own. Doctor, do you know which android it was?"

Oksana nodded.

"As you know, macromolecules contain the individual's code. We have already identified the Companion who matches the macromolecules found on the coordinator's clothes."

"Well?"

Oksana hesitated and bent her head helplessly.

"Sorry, Etta," she said pitifully. "It was Raul."

Etta jumped up from her seat, tipping over the chair she was sitting on.

"But that's impossible! Raul wouldn't hurt anyone!"

"But those were his molecules we found on the deceased's clothes. There is no mistake. If he can explain it, he's in no danger."

"How could he explain it?" someone from the back row of chairs said, snorting. "If he killed, he won't admit it."

"Why meditate on it? If he is dangerous, we have to get rid of him," Dr. Celina Xiao added. "Deactivate him now, there will be time to investigate later."

"Over my dead body, do you understand?!" Etta shouted. "Over my dead body!"

"Calm down everyone!" Captain Willner hit his hands on the table. "Ms. Wysocka, can you say with full confidence that the android Raul is guilty of murder?"

"Of course not, I haven't said that! Only that the molecules with his marker have been found on the deceased's shirt."

"So how to explain that?" Dr. Xiao started again, but the captain silenced her with an angry glance. He knew how to control people and this skill now proved very useful to him. He was dealing with an agitated crew, an unexplained murderer, and a suspect who was a very comfortable scapegoat for some. As the people quieted slightly, he pointed to one of the detectives, giving him a right to speak.

"We do not know if he killed the coordinator. We only now know that for some reason he struggled with the coordinator, and we must clarify whether it led to something more." Erik Karlson got up from his seat. "Everyone, please go back to your tasks now. Major, you will find and bring Raul 209C to the hearing."

Etta took a deep breath. She didn't want to use Easyhal in public, and on top of that, in this situation. Suddenly, she remembered something.

"If so, please arrest me!" she cried with determination. "The law states that the Dominant is responsible for the offense committed by his android."

Detective Karlson approached her to put his hand on her shoulder reassuringly.

"Calm down, Miss Solis," he said. "I understand you are upset, but we have to look at this clue before we divert suspicion in another direction."

"You believe it was Raul who killed Colonel Nakamara, don't you?"

"I, Miss Solis, don't have a view on this matter. For now, I am just collecting all possible data. I can assure you that Raul will be treated the same as any other interrogated person. Anyway, you will be present at the interrogation."

"Can I?"

"You have to. An android can't be interrogated without the presence of his Dominant."

This news didn't calm Etta, her heart still beat like crazy. But she felt a bit less uncertain. She went obediently to the interrogation room assigned by the investigative team, and took a big breath. Paradoxically, here, in this small group, she felt more exposed to the fire than in the packed meeting room. And yet no one was her enemy here.

*****

Two soldiers from the patrol brought Raul to the office. He behaved normally, as usual. He didn't show any sign of anxiety, even within the destabilization pattern, about which Etta recently read in the textbook.

"Sit down," the detective said, pointing at a chair. Raul sat down obediently, giving only a quick, almost imperceptible glance at his Domina.

The detective leaned his elbows on the table and looked at the suspect carefully—more of a habit than the real need, for there was nothing to be read from the behavior of the android.

"What is your name?" he asked.

"Raul 209C."

"How old are you?"

"Eight months, three weeks, and two days."

"Who is your Dominant?"

"Miss Estrella Katerina Solis."

"Where were you on the morning of July 2nd of this year, between midnight and 3 a.m., when Kurt Nakamara was assassinated?"

"In our quarters, with my Domina."

"You didn't leave the apartment?"

The android was silent for a moment.

"Reply," Etta urged him.

"I left."

"Why?" Karlson continued.

A long silence and then sudden words, "I will not answer this question."

"Why?"

"Because I left on private business."

"What private business can a robot have?" Carter snorted. Gongadze silenced him with a hiss, and Karlson didn't even notice his words. All the time he was focused on the black-haired android, who was sitting in front of him with his face still and his hands on his lap.

"You apparently don't understand that this is an investigation into a murder. We need to know where you were."

"I refuse to answer."

"Raul," Etta groaned with horror. Her Companion looked at her in his characteristic, gentle way.

"I didn't do anything wrong," he said. "I did not kill anyone."

"Maybe you didn't want to do it. You two struggled, you are very strong and maybe, by accident…" Karlson suggested.

"It didn't happen. I never touched the chief coordinator. That night, I wasn't in his office."

"But we need to know what you did that night, even if it wasn't anything wrong," the detective pressed patiently. It was evident that he had experience in interrogating androids and that he had no prejudice against them.

"Raul, please."

The android was silent, clenching his lips tightly. Dr. O'Leary, who had taken the role of an observer so far, now coughed slightly.

"May I ask you for a moment to the room next door?" he asked.

Tengiz Gongadze nodded.

"Watch him," he said to the soldiers. Together with the detectives and Etta, who was on the verge of crying, they left the room, following the cybernetician, who first closed the door carefully then glanced around the room as if looking for wiretaps.

"This is a tough case," he said at last. "I haven't yet encountered a situation in which a Companion would refuse a Dominant's request. However, Raul is a very advanced individual.

I can't say how advanced, because I haven't done proper tests, but it seems to me that he either has extra circuits, or he learned to use the ones he owns in a specific way. I don't think we can trust everything he is telling us."

"Raul doesn't lie!" Etta protested sharply. The betrayal of the man she had already started to considered a friend hurt her so much that she lost her breath. O'Leary looked at her briefly with his faded eyes.

"You can't know that for sure," he said emphatically. "You said yourself he's not a machine, he's a self-conscious being… that is, he isn't limited by anything. People usually have a completely false idea about it, maybe they simply don't want to know the truth."

"And what is the truth?" Carter asked skeptically, crossing his arms over his chest. His whole stoic, squat figure expressed disbelief.

"Androids can lie and nothing really prevents them from doing so. No warrant or prohibition derived from the program. They don't do it just because they don't see logic in it. But suppose Raul found a logical justification?"

"So what?" the lieutenant colonel asked. "Do you think he is guilty?"

"I didn't say that. And frankly, I don't like this idea. But I think we can't exclude it. He admitted that he did leave his quarters. Probably nobody saw him, otherwise we would have it in the report. Meanwhile…"

He touched the screen on the table.

"Please take a look. Five people were registered in the street within the time window of interest to us. We know the route of each of them, and none of them were even near the center. If Raul left in those hours, he had to show a huge skill of camouflage, one unheard of in androids. Great cunning, in human terms. If he killed Nakamara, he must be absolutely deactivated, because he is more dangerous than we might guess. However"—here the doctor raised his hand, stopping Etta's violent protest—"we can't blame him and rub our hands in satisfaction. We must have the real killer, no matter who it is."

"Miss Solis, what was the nature of your contacts with the deceased?" Major Carter turned to Etta.

"Normal! If you don't trust me, give me a truth serum. In fact, I demand it!" the girl screamed angrily, struggling not to slap the unpleasant investigator in the face. She would be delighted to leave a mark of all her nails on his hideous mug... but in spite of everything, she was too sensible to behave so hysterically.

Erik Karlson sighed with some weariness.

"Miss Solis, we have already interrogated you," he said gently. "The serum of truth was sprayed in the air. You couldn't have lied, unless you had been properly conditioned beforehand. However, I have reviewed your file and I know that this is unlikely in your case. You have been here too long, and this type of conditioning stops working after a maximum of two months."

Etta opened her mouth and closed it without a word. There was no point in saying anything, everything was clear. She suddenly felt like an object in someone else's hands and preferred to keep silent so as not to blurt out something unnecessarily.

Dr. O'Leary, who was looking at her with compassion all this time, continued, "You know very well that Raul is capable of being brutal to someone who is a threat to you. We can even assume that he feels something like jealousy. Thus we have to take into account that he could have killed. That alone wouldn't be so terrifying, not more than, for example, a traffic accident. However, this crime has been planned and executed perfectly, and that can be scary."

"Doctor, to the point. Do you think the androids can try to harm humanity?" Gongadze asked harshly, ignoring Etta's growing irritation.

"It wouldn't be logical. They know well that in the event of a crash, only a person can help them. And they can't reproduce. Due to the Karpinsky Principle, an android may have access to every bit of knowledge except the one that relates to his own construction. In this way, many dangers have been eliminated, starting from the undesirable growth of the population of our Companions. An android could build another android, but he won't do it because he can't access sensitive data."

Suddenly, raised voices could be heard outside the door. One of them was undoubtedly the voice of Veronica. The rest belonged to the guards, who didn't want to let the girl into the interrogation room. Tengiz Gongadze frowned, then walked to the door and opened it wide.

"What is going on?" he asked sharply.

Veronica looked very agitated. Her uniform was unbuttoned and her hair messy, she was red in face, and her eyes glowed frantically.

"Colonel, I have to tell you something," she choked out.

"Get your uniform in order first, Lieutenant! An officer shouldn't stand before the commander in such a state!"

The girl followed the order hastily and straightened officially.

"I am asking for permission to report information relevant for the investigation."

"Come in."

Veronica hurried into the room, where everyone looked at her with unquestioned curiosity. As soon as Gongadze closed the door, she fired out, "I know why something struck me as odd when I saw the body of the coordinator. Something didn't seem right and I didn't know what at the time. Now I have realized what it was."

"So?" Major Carter urged her.

"He was in somebody else's shirt."

"Are you sure about that?"

"Absolutely. He never had one like that."

"How well did you know the coordinator that you feel capable of making this statement?" Erik Karlson asked.

"We were lovers for some time," the girl replied calmly. "I knew his wardrobe well, and as I said—that shirt wasn't his."

The detective rubbed his unshaved chin and thought deeply. It didn't make much sense... why would the chief coordinator put on somebody else's shirt, particularly in the middle of the night while working in the office on secret reports? And how was it related to the murder? The faces of the others clearly pointed out that they didn't know how to interpret this new evidence, either.

"Wait a minute," Etta said. "Dr. O'Leary, are you thinking of the same thing as me?"

MacLean tapped his fingers lightly on the back of the chair next to him. "Of course," he said grimly. "But that complicates matters, and more so than you think."

"What is going on?" the lieutenant colonel asked roughly.

As briefly as possible, the doctor described the conversation he had with Etta and the revelations she had shared with him. Then she herself described the incident with her brother-in-law, trying not to miss anything. She had no idea what grudge Dario might have with Kurt Nakamara, but he certainly hated androids—he would have been willing to implicate Raul even without another reason, not to mention to spite the cousin who turned him down. She also mentioned that Dario had belonged to the movement of the Peoplists, although she emphasized that as a member of this organization, the young Cantoralle did not commit any crime. The investigative group listened to her quietly, contemplating this new clue.

"So there was aggressive behavior toward the insistent colonist, right?" Major Carter asked.

"Raul acted in my defense," stressed Etta with emphasis.

"I've never heard of anything like that. And you, Mr. O'Leary?" the major asked the doctor and without waiting for an answer, went on. "So your android isn't as gentle and innocent as you have been trying to convince us. But there is one more doubt—are the two incidents connected?"

"We could be sure if we knew what your brother-in-law was wearing that day," Karlson supported him.

"It was dark," Etta stammered, realizing that she didn't really remember that detail. Dario was wearing a shirt, but what did it look like?

"Interrogate him, just like me and others," she insisted angrily.

"If he is conditioned, we won't find out anything anyway. He arrived here just three weeks ago, right? So it is very possible that if he was conditioned, he will still be immune to the truth serum for at least five more weeks. He will deny everything and we will be back to square one."

"But if it's him, then letting him continue his actions can be very risky," Veronica noted. She had already calmed down and smoothed her untidy hair.

Dr. O'Leary tapped on the chair again, this time harder.

"There is a way," he said. "But before I say it, I have to ask everyone to keep things strictly confidential, as it is a production secret."

"I think we all know when we need to keep our mouths shut," Tengiz Gongadze said harshly. "Please tell us, Doctor."

"Every android built in the manufactory has a special recorder sewn in, which records everything the object sees and hears. A kind of black box. We keep it in secrecy mainly because of the androids themselves, because the knowledge that they carry a spy would interfere with their individual development and could cause a desire to get rid of the implant. And that could be fatal. I am able to remove the recorder from Raul's body and read the data from that unfortunate day."

"Why didn't you say this before? We would know if he was guilty without the interrogation!"

"I kept quiet, because this android, especially as advanced as he is, is not a doll. How would you respond to the news that someone is watching you day and night? If I had to, I would have done it in the end, but until now I'd hoped that we would find out the truth in other ways."

At this point, Etta realized what else had to be recorded in Raul's recorder, and blushed. Veronica, more controlled, made only an indistinct grunt.

"So there is no choice, we have to do it," Karlson decided firmly.

O'Leary nodded, though it was obvious that this issue bothered him. He felt guilty, as if he had betrayed his own children and couldn't help seeing things this way.

"I will tell him about it." Etta got up from the chair, already calm and composed. "I don't suppose he will take it well."

She already knew that this was going to humiliate Raul, and she was wondering how to alleviate the blow. Cool logic was not her strongest side. She more often followed her gut feeling, and now she felt her android would have difficulty accepting the fact that he had been equipped with a recorder. True enough, it could now save him from very serious consequences—the murder charge was, after all, a real threat, and at best, they would be separated for a long time—but being aware of having such device in his body would be definitely difficult for Raul. She couldn't spare him, he had to know. But it would be better if he learned about it from her.

XI

I t is difficult to predict the reactions of a nonlinear being. It is even more difficult to define them correctly, because the actions of the androids are entirely under their control—they don't reflect anything they don't intend to show. They don't have a heart rate that can accelerate, they do not breathe, so they don't catch air spasmodically like humans, and have no human blood vessels or blood, so they neither become pale nor red. However, Raul's polymeric eyes started to vibrate from left to right, something Etta had never seen him do before. He stood up from his chair, clenching his hands in a human motion. He was quiet for a moment, then suddenly raised his hands and threw out a real torrent of hard-to-understand, hardly separated, monotonous words, among which the girl finally caught the repeating words:

"I don't want, I don't want, I don't want, Take it away, I don't agree—"

"Raul, calm down!" she yelled. "Dr. O'Leary will remove the recorder and check only that event, nothing else, I promise you that! Calm down, my friend."

She took his hands, sensing artificial muscles in his arm hardened like a stone under the smooth fabric of the clothes. The mode of action in the brain of her Companion had to jump to the highest level of readiness and it had to be addressed as soon as possible.

"Recorders are not meant to control you, only to protect you," MacLean O'Leary said. He had followed Etta into the examination room. "Stop making up these ideas. If I treated you as you think I am doing, I would have just shut your mind off before removing the implant and you never even would have known about it. I assure you that I have enough knowledge and resources to do that. But I consider you a being, not an object, that's why I agreed we had to tell you."

"I don't want to have it."

"Okay, so we won't put it back. Happy?"

"You had no right to equip us with something like that. It's unethical."

"Yes, that's true," O'Leary said. "But why are you so uncomfortable with this? Logically, you should consider having a recorder a successful circumstance as it will help prove your innocence. Otherwise it might be difficult."

Raul slowly released the tension in his body. It was evident that the violent protest was a spontaneous reaction from him, and he was now trying to analyze why he'd reacted like that.

"You should ask us," he said finally. "Not do this secretly. Secrets are bad. You have to speak straight and give us a choice. Doctor, we are not programmed, we think."

"I know it best. Because there are only three of us here, I am going to confess that I belong to the 'A.I. Free' organization, which is fighting for the widening of androids' rights. Believe me, I'm the last man to want to see you enslaved."

Raul was silent for a moment, his eyes fixed at one point. At that moment, he really resembled a perfectly made mannequin, but after a few seconds he twitched imperceptibly, looked at the doctor and asked, "When and where will you do it?"

"In the data processing room. We will go there together with the detectives and Lieutenant Colonel Gongadze."

The android nodded slightly. "So let's do it as soon as possible."

On the way, O'Leary drew a small scanner from his pocket and turned the reader toward Raul. He looked intensely at the changing readings resembling a spectral analysis.

"It doesn't make any sense," he muttered finally, and when he raised his head, his eyes were burning. "Raul, can you describe the moment you started feeling an undesirable electrical destabilization?"

Polymeric eyes turned toward O'Leary.

"A few times before we came here. They increased during training. It depends on the circumstances. Sometimes I feel the alternating current... here."

He put his hand on his chest, where his mechanical heart was hidden—a self-sufficient battery. The doctor shook his head, still staring at the readings.

"It's unusual. Unbelievable. The institute laughed at me when I mentioned that possibility. Everything is one hundred percent efficient, no malfunction, neither from the factory nor acquired, nothing to blame for this anomaly."

"Doctor...?" Etta touched his shoulder. He looked at her triumphantly.

"You don't understand? If he doesn't want something, then depending on the severity of his resistance, the electric charge increases. It is the exact equivalent of human emotions. I've predicted that something like that could form, but my dissertation was rejected."

"Is it bad?"

"Not yet. He can deactivate an undesirable charge. However, the mere fact that it exists and cause discomfort indicates the development unforeseen by science and technology. Well, and no one knows what it will lead to."

The excitement of the doctor was kind of unseemly under these circumstances. He probably realized it, because he finally put away the scanner and reached for the communicator.

"Leo, please come to the control center, interrogation room. Bring the kit for minor androsurgical interventions with you," he said.

Etta realized with some surprise that she hadn't seen the cybernetician's deputy before. She knew his name was Leonard Derkacz and that he was almost as brilliant as O'Leary, but she had not seen him. Allegedly, he worked conceptually. Unlike other residents of the center, he didn't leave his studio, and didn't participate in meetings or trainings. If not for his name on the list of employees, nobody would even know of his existence.

"Is he necessary here?" Major Carter asked with visible discontent.

"Unfortunately, yes," the doctor replied harshly. "Removing the recorder requires the cooperation of two people that know the procedure."

"More and more complications," the detective murmured, and it was clear from his face that he didn't believe that the android accused of the crime wasn't guilty. In his view, all Dr. O'Leary's activities were a mere waste of time, but since Lieutenant General Gongadze had agreed to it…

Leonard Derkacz appeared in the interrogation room ten minutes later. At the sight of him, Etta raised her eyebrows in silent astonishment. While MacLean O'Leary looked bizarre, his assistant beat all records in that respect. Almost six and a half feet tall, skinny as a skeleton, slightly hunched, he was dressed in a blue sweatshirt and old pants with unnecessarily wide legs that fluttered around his ankles. His longish head was covered with glistening black hair, which looked as if it had been lacquered and glued to his skull. The bony face with sharp features seemed to be composed of elements from two different sets. A beautifully arched forehead and a prominent, slightly eagle-like nose of an aristocratic line were somehow in disharmony with an elongated jaw with a flat chin, small ugly lips, and narrow eyes hiding under the bushy eyebrows. Large protruding ears would probably make even a much nicer face ugly, although they weren't surprising on Leonard. It was impossible to tell his age—there was the impression that he'd looked the same as a teenager and he would look the same as an old man. Still, he looked likeable. Etta thought immediately that he had to be a good man, though certainly a big freak. What else could be expected from MacLean O'Leary assistant, anyway?

"I hope it's something important," he said coldly, placing a small messenger bag on the table. His voice was deep and dark.

"More than you think," O'Leary said, and described the situation briefly.

Derkacz listened without interruption, and only when the doctor finished, said with calm condemnation in his voice, "You mean you've destroyed the effects of many years work in a single moment? Congratulations."

"Drop that sarcasm, Leo. Let's just get to work."

"As you want, MacLean, but don't blame me if things go wrong. An android without supervision is asking for trouble."

"I'm here," Raul suddenly said. It sounded like a reproach.

Leonard looked at him with astonishment. "What?"

"I'm here. I hear and understand."

O'Leary let out a quick laugh. He looked very pleased that someone managed to surprise his assistant, who for his part seemed to be quite dumbfounded.

"What's so funny for you, MacLean? I haven't yet seen the response of the 'offended dignity' type in any nonlinear beings. I know that they think for themselves, but this is already starting to look like human emotions. This is not funny."

"For me it is."

"And for me not, because we don't know how far the escalation will go. They could get out of control."

The doctor shook his head pitifully.

"Leo, when will you get it in your stubborn head that they have never been under our control? They are not lathes but conscious beings, thinking independently."

His assistant waved his hand dismissively and changed the subject, "Are you taking the right or left side?"

"Left. Give me scalpel number six and bigger tweezers."

"Don't hurt him," Etta blurted out. Both men looked at her with a mixture of amazement and offense.

"No worries, miss," O'Leary grunted, getting to work. The detectives and lieutenant colonel watched their actions no less carefully than Etta, without talking, even trying not to breathe so as not to disturb the two scholars during their precise work. It turned out that the procedure was not as simple as they had thought—before its removal, the recorder had to be disconnected from a series of microscopic wires, each of which had to be closed first and then its cut coating fixed. Raul sat motionless, surrendering to all that with a fatalistic resignation. Finally, the recorder—a tiny thing resembling an ordinary capsule—was on the table.

"Now we just need to connect..." O'Leary opened the computer panel on the table and started rummaging through it. Raul stood up, shook his head slightly, as if to see if everything was all right, walked over to Etta, and wrapped his arms around her. He was already composed, calm as always, but the doctor had the vague impression that for some reason he was in need of that touch, the feeling that he wasn't alone. It wasn't the first time he had seen anything like it, but it still amazed him. Nobody had expected such a strong bond between Companions and their Dominants, but it did exist. The stronger the bond, the lower the IQ of the android. But even the wisest of them weren't able to break that bond, as if their Dominant was someone their own existence was based on. This wasn't an objective truth, but the androids themselves saw it this way, and it still remained a mystery why. One thing seemed certain, that this type of suggestion didn't exist in the core program.

"Okay, ready," the doctor finally stated, activating the preview. The words "PLAYBACK: CHOOSE AN OPTION" appeared on the paper-thin monitor. O'Leary glanced at the still android.

"Don't be afraid, Raul. I promised you something, didn't I?" he said harshly. "Miss Solis, when did the incident with your brother-in-law happen?"

"On June 30th, sometime between 10 p.m. and midnight. I know it's a long time window, but I really don't remember exactly. It was after we got out from the meeting that evening."

"That's fine." The doctor ran his fingers over the keyboard, setting the date and time, and then activated the image scrolling.

For the first time, Etta had the opportunity to look at the world through Raul's eyes. First of all, she was amazed by the extraordinary resolution and depth of the recorded image—it was truly perfect, perfect to the limit. Someone put in a lot of effort, inventiveness, and dreadfully expensive technology to create this tiny device, that for Raul was nothing more than the iron collar of a slave from the old days. She understood what he felt, especially that it was also humiliating for her to see the whole team of investigators watching this embarrassing incident with Dario. She tried to keep her expression neutral, but she felt her cheeks burning like fire, though there was no fault of hers in the whole incident. She was looking at the screen from the corner of her eye, but she still noticed something she had missed before—Raul shook Dario a lot harder than was necessary. Watching the incident from his perspective, it was easy to notice that he could have just pushed the insistent man away. She hoped no one else would notice it.

Dr. O'Leary quickly copied the part of the recording that was interesting to him to two separate media devices, one of which he handed to Leonard.

"Give it to the technicians and let them determine the texture, the color, the weave, and whatever else they come up with," he said. "I'm going to the medical section. I have to check something else."

He took the recorder out of the computer and put it on Raul's palm.

"It's yours. You can keep it or destroy it, as you like."

"Doctor!" Carter cried out in protest, but O'Leary just looked at him ironically, and the major shut up, disconcerted by that look for some reason.

"You are free," Tengiz Gongadze said to Etta. "And your Companion, too, but please watch him. He is not allowed to leave your quarters until he receives a rescindment of that order."

"Yes, sir," Etta replied. She felt immense relief that she could finally get out of here, to go back with Raul to their assigned apartment, and to vent her despair in private. She needed that, although she realized why only after leaving the control center. The discovery that the probable killer of the coordinator was Dario, her former friend, adolescent love object, and current brother-in-law, had shaken her deeply. Never before had she experienced such a grim moment and she simply had to cry in order to come to terms with it. Easyhal wouldn't do any good right now.

In her quarters, Etta sat down on the bed and sobbed for nearly half an hour, while Raul sat next to her and stroked her head in a monotonous motion.

"Come on, calm down," he said at last. "Forgive me that I have behaved so... disorderly. When I heard about the recorder, I felt for a moment as if the data in my memory banks had been scattered. I couldn't sort them."

Etta squeezed his arm, sensing under her fingers the smoothness of the cyberskin and the small muscles of his hand responsible for the movements of the phalanges. The muscles of the androids reflected human ones in every detail, so that holding their limbs felt identical as touching a living person. The only difference was that there were no tremors in an android's skin and muscles. Their bodies were still and calm. Maybe that's why she felt so good by Raul's side.

"I'm going to calm down," she promised. "But for now, I have to cry. For people, it is a way to discharge emotions."

"Discharge? As with the battery?"

"In a sense, yes. Imagine an overcharged battery... if no current is drained from it, it will destroy the device. And if a man doesn't drain away excess emotions, he may get sick, even seriously."

Raul nodded seriously.

"That's why we were taught how to relieve people from the tensions associated with their reproductive biology. We were shown movies and it was said that for people it is very important. Am I... doing it right?"

Etta blushed. The directness of artificial intelligence was sometimes really embarrassing.

"I have no complaints," she said evasively. "Let's not talk about it, please."

"I'm doing my best. It wasn't unpleasant to you, was it?"

"Please understand, these things are very particular for people. I don't like talking about it."

"I don't understand, but I surrender. I am your Companion, I will do what you want."

Etta wiped away her tears. This was a problem she wasn't able to solve yet—on the one hand, she enjoyed having a very devoted being on her side, and on the other, she didn't want Raul to be her slave. She wanted him to want to be with her, of his own free will. But she didn't know how to be sure of his feelings. How to distinguish what an android must do from what he wants to do? She didn't know it was possible at all, but she very much wanted to find out.

*****

Leonard woke his boss at five in the morning.

"The technicians confirmed the android's version," he said. "They checked the record with all available methods and there is no doubt that the coordinator was wearing the shirt of a man in the recording."

"I had no doubt about it," O'Leary muttered sleepily, and turned on his other side. "Give the results immediately to the lieutenant colonel and those wannabe Sherlocks."

"Immediately?"

"Of course. I don't want to be the only moron you woke up because of this."

His assistant shook his head but followed his boss's command. He was accustomed to his unconventional way of being and his peculiar theories, which he didn't always share. They had their love of the androids in common, but they didn't agree in their opinions on the possibility of developing artificial intelligence. Leonard admired the perfection of the androids, but he didn't treat them like humans, while O'Leary saw them as almost equal to people. They had argued about this more than once, but neither of them had succeeded in convincing the other yet.

At approximately six o'clock in the morning, a patrol of soldiers entered the house where the Cantoralles were staying and they took Dario just like they found him—in pajamas and barefoot. Ten minutes later, Nayeli was at Etta's and was choking with hysterical crying, alternately asking for her help, accusing her of jealousy, and reminding her of their relationship.

Etta finally forced her to use the Easyhal inhaler and then said sharply, "Pull yourself together. Go home and take care of the children. Your husband committed a serious crime and I certainly won't defend him. Moreover, I hope that even if they don't euthanize him, they will lock him up and throw the key away."

Despite the relaxing medication, Nayeli burst out again, "It's all a lie! And you're the one to blame…"

She flooded Etta with a stream of some unclear explanations, mixed with desperate accusations, and finally she got to such a state that she tried to hit her sister. It caused Raul to intervene in the quarrel, trying to stop the mad woman with logical, calm words. But this had just the opposite effect.

"This is some defender you have here!" Nayeli called viciously as the android stood between them, preventing her from punching her sister. "You couldn't find a guy with blood and bones, so you got yourself a doll! That's the only thing you can do, because no man will even consider you!"

"Raul is an android, not a doll. And he's twice as human as Dario," Etta said, trying to stay quiet and calm. "Calm down already, you crazy woman! You won't get anywhere acting like that!"

Unfortunately, her words did not come to fruition and the girl finally had to call a medical team who took the hysterical Nayeli to the clinic.

"What will happen to her now?" Raul asked when they were finally alone.

"Do you care?"

"I think so. She's your sister."

"I don't think she will be allowed to stay here. She will probably be sent to Montepietro, together with the children. I don't think she knows anything, but they won't risk leaving her at the center… let alone taking her with the expedition."

"Considering all the pros and cons, it may be better for her," he said after a moment. "She won't be exposed to the unpredictable dangers of the migration. She will be in good hands. After all, the doctors will take care of her."

"Sure."

The android embraced her gently and hugged her. Nevertheless, Etta felt bad. The clash with Nayeli had put her off balance, because although she thought her sister was definitely stupid, in a way she loved her and had remembered her all those years when they were far away from each other. But she had known her as a nice, cheerful child, and now fate sent her an adult woman apparently under the strong influence of a despotic husband, and actually unable to think for herself. This whole situation was really unpleasant. She solved it by taking an extra dose of Easyhal and going back to bed.

It was late in the afternoon when she and Raul were called to the training center. Dr. Xiao's assistant had to call her through the intercom because, due to her worries, Etta had forgotten that they had to attend the special meeting. She appeared in the conference room breathless, her hair still wet from her shower, and very embarrassed by her forgetfulness.

"Well, finally everybody is here," Dr. O'Leary stated as they walked into the room. "Raul, you sit down with your team. Miss Solis, please come to the front."

Confused and upset, Etta sat timidly between Leonard Derkacz and data processing manager, a Nigerian woman named Iman Gossip. She had no idea what this was all about, and it was impossible to deduce from the faces of the people around her. Apart from them, the front seating area also included Veronica, Dr. Berent, a biotechnologist, and Lieutenant Rod Denberry, the deputy head of protection. A bit further down sat the Dominators of the androids gathered in the rooms, three female models of a blond Venus type, and four much more varied male models.

"Everyone," O'Leary began. "We have come here to discuss a very important issue. During the crisis we have just dealt with, I was forced to reveal a construction detail of the new generation of androids. I am referring here to a recorder, acting as a black box. The violent reaction of Raul 209C, who is here with us, made me realize that the use of these modules is morally ambiguous. On the one hand, we recognize the full independence of artificial intelligence, while on the other hand, we install in them a system that tracks all the actions of the beings we have created. It's not quite all right. I suggest that we allow our Companions to make individual decisions about keeping or deleting their modules."

"Is that reasonable?" Lieutenant Denberry asked skeptically. "After all, you have proven that such a recorder can be very useful."

"Of course, but people are not equipped with such devices unless they want to be. In my opinion, the androids should also be able to choose whether they want to be freer or safer."

"Absurd," Dr. Berent muttered dismissively. Leonard, who was sitting beside Etta, stood up.

"Maybe we should hear what our Companions say about it," he suggested. "Roy 98D, please."

Roy, an android with a typical Asian appearance, shook his head.

"I have nothing to say," he said stiffly. "In my opinion, this question is irrelevant. I rely on the judgment of my Domina."

"Rhonda 12F?"

"Me too."

"Rasmus 101A?"

"Please remove this module, regardless of Miss Hornet's opinion."

"Ruslana 39F?"

"I have no objections."

"Rosamunde 305F?"

"Please remove it."

"Roger 7E?"

"Please leave it." The tiny, curly blond android with the pink cheeks of a cherub and green eyes continued, giving his reason, "Better to have proof of one's innocence or someone else's fault. No court will believe our words."

Leonard turned to the people gathered in the hall.

"You have heard them. The views of the androids vary in this regard, and that in itself proves that we have to consider their opinion if we don't want to fall into the role of slave owners. That would mean for us to step back in social development by three or even four civilization epochs."

"I don't understand the problem. Since they are just machines—" Dr. Berent started to say, apparently deciding to express her views on this issue. Etta had never liked the woman, arrogant and filled with self-importance, but now she felt a huge aversion to her.

"They are not just machines," O'Leary interrupted coldly. "They are built in a factory, but they are independent minds, capable of making spontaneous decisions. They respond to stressful situations and are able to feel a kind of equivalent to human emotions. We must not act against them unethically. My team and I decided that those of the Companions who reported their desire to get rid of the implant, would be operated on and their recorders destroyed."

Not everyone present in the room shared the doctor's enthusiasm, but after a short discussion, they signed a joint statement on the matter.

On that day, Etta also learned that Dario had been taken to the highest security prison and Nayeli was to be expelled from the center. On the one hand, she was very sorry, but on the other, she was relieved. The presence of her sister was getting on her nerves more than she wanted to admit. She felt a pressure because of her, and so far she had been trying to steer clear of Nayeli. Despite this, her sense of duty made her go to the hospital to see her sister before moving. Later she decided that it had not been a good idea—Nayeli was soaked with sedatives, her eyes were wild and mad, and she looked like a stranger.

"Why did you come?" she snapped, seeing Etta. "You want to calm your conscience? You couldn't have Dario for yourself, so you ruined my marriage?!"

"You know that is not the case. Dario killed Coordinator Nakamara and tried to blame Raul for it—"

"You will do anything to protect your mechanical toy, won't you?!" Nayeli shouted as she threw herself on the glass separating them. "You do it because you know that machine won't leave you like the others! You are a zero! You are nobody! Zeroes are only good for sex! Nobody wants you and nobody ever will!"

She hit the glass with her hands, screaming, and scared, Etta finally pressed the alarm button. The two paramedics rushed into the box, dragged the fighting woman away from the window, and then Doctor Leveroux, who was in charge of the ward, appeared.

"Please go now, Miss Solis," she said to Etta. "I know you wanted to do well, but your sister is in a state in which nothing gets through to her."

"Is it a disease?" Etta asked, trembling.

"Probably only a temporary breakdown, but only time will tell. Please don't visit her anymore. Apparently, she is now blaming you for her misfortune, so it is better for her not to see you. Later she will get over it."

Etta also thought it would be better. She felt guilty, absurdly guilty for what happened to Nayeli, and she was tormented by a sense of helplessness. She couldn't help her sister—the worst thing was that she didn't believe the doctor. She heard a false note in her voice, and that meant that Nayeli might be considered mentally ill. If the committee assessed her state as unpromising to return to full health, the euthanasia procedure would be implemented and no one would dare to protest, even their parents. That was the law. Usually she understood the law and accepted it without reservation, but now it was extremely difficult. She tried to look logically at what had happened but couldn't. She felt as if someone hit her hard on her head, or even as if she had been battered in a serious fight. Her whole body was in pain, and although she was aware that it was just nerves, she didn't feel any better.

When she got back to her quarters, Raul didn't asked anything. He helped the girl take off her uniform, then took her to the shower. Seeing that she was too shaken to even hold the sponge in her hand, he gently took it from her and helped her wash, like one would help a baby. Then he wrapped her in a large towel, took her in his arms, and carried her to bed.

XII

D r. O'Leary and his assistant were working on the project of the direct visualization of the readings, when Etta came to their lab with Raul. Both scientists looked at them with visible astonishment. The whole center knew that their lab was "Comanche land", as Captain Willner used to say, and that meant everyone was to steer clear of this section. For some reason, Etta Solis and her Companion decided to cross into the forbidden zone.

"What is going on?" Leonard asked, openly impatient.

"Because of the closure of my brother-in-law's case..." Etta began, then she fell silent. This introduction seemed to her awkward and even stupid, especially since both men had an almost hostile look on their faces. Raul helped her.

"Because you acted honestly, letting us remove the recorders, I decided to say what I did that night."

"Good, but why to us? Isn't it better to tell the lieutenant colonel? It seems that in spite of everything, he still doesn't quite trust you," O'Leary said after a long moment. It was evident that he was very surprised, no less than his assistant.

"No, not better. This is something I have to say to you, because you are an android specialist. You will know how to help."

"To help whom?"

"Don't look at me," Etta said. "That's his business, not mine."

Raul explained the issue patiently, in plain words, and before he even finished, both of his listeners were astounded. The story was as amazing as it was unprecedented.

A year ago, a tragedy happened in the neighborhood of the Cantoralles' house. A young man, Guillermo Hernan, disappeared in quite unclear circumstances. Because his body wasn't found, and neither any trails nor clues, his case was still open and the police did not intend to close it. Sometime later, Dario Cantoralle left Montepietro for two months, allegedly to carry out a corporate order. On this trip, using Hernan's documents, he received the Companion ordered by the lost man, Raina 18B. For several months he had been trying to train her to become an assassin. When he didn't succeed, he changed his mind and carried out a series of experiments of unclear purpose on her. When his family got the order to leave for the colonist center, he locked the crippled android in the basement of their home and left her to her own fate. Using the circuits of her own arm, Raina constructed an electronic picklock, managed to open the door somehow, and then set out to follow her Dominant. Why she did that, she couldn't explain. In fact, it wasn't easy to understand what she was saying at all. Dario didn't care about her mental development and in some aspects, she was like a child. In any case, she had somehow reached the migration center, although no one understood how she managed to cross the line of sensors. She was found by the rescue team under Raul's command, which was just leaving for exercises. The androids hid Raina in an unused room in a warehouse and tried to repair her damages. That was what Raul was busy with on the night of the murder.

"Wait a minute. And how did you know what to do?" Leonard interrupted.

"From the textbook. Etta borrowed it from Dr. O'Leary, and I copied it for my use," the android explained.

Derkacz looked at his boss, and his narrow lips twitched in a grimace of slight surprise.

"It's getting more and more unusual," he said, and turned to Raul. "You have committed a crime, do you know that? That knowledge is off limits for androids."

"I will not use it for the wrong purposes. I wanted to help Raina."

"Easy, Leo. As far as I can remember, I let Miss Solis borrow *Andropology* by Ludovic. That textbook doesn't have information on the most important parts, only the data on the outer shell," Dr. O'Leary said, and at the same time he was taking tools, diagnostic scanners, and spokes of various sizes, filled with artificial skin components, out of a drawer and packing them in a briefcase. "But Raul, you have to understand that just like there is knowledge not accessible to most people, there are also things that you and the other Companions don't have the right to know. There is a reason for it and it must be respected, even if we don't like it."

"Yes, Doctor. I promise I won't do it again," the android said obediently. "It is not my intention to cause trouble for anyone."

"Well, show us the way, brave knight."

*****

The warehouses were on the outer edge of the center. They were built quite a long time ago and on quite a big scale, so they could be used in the event of a cataclysm. The aboveground complex was complemented by solid cellars made of reinforced concrete, able to even withstand a nearby atomic explosion. Typically, this complex was used for storage, but not all of it. The android transformed one of the rooms of an unused section into something like a one-person lazarette for their friend. It was evident that they were not guided by logic or functionality while arranging this place, and that was already strange. Although the construction of each android allowed him to lie down in any conditions without a problem, one of them brought Raina a mattress and bedding, a pillow under her head, even a blanket—it had grown colder recently, but the thought that someone wanted to protect an android from the cold seemed funny. It could simply be that the blanket was provided for the purchase of covering her, since her clothes, the standard blue coverall suit given to androids in the factory, torn and stiff from the dirt, was lying next to her. The inorganic patient also had a player and a several books, but they were most shocked by the sight of a tin mug of water, into which someone had put flowers stolen from the park: two carnations, an aster, and several twigs of flowering freesia.

"Are you sure there were no other people here before us?" Dr. O'Leary asked, looking suspiciously at Raul.

"I am sure. You are the first."

"Then where did the flowers come from?"

"Rasmus brought them. Is it… wrong?"

"I would say it's fascinating," Leonard muttered, and the doctor shrugged his shoulders, not sure how to comment.

The android lying on the makeshift bed seemed to be in a catatonic state. She was of a different type than the female Companions in the center, without exception tall blondes with blue eyes and pink lips. Like all the androids of that popular template, they had a common description, although specially programmed statistical deviations in production made it so they weren't identical to each other. They differed in facial angle, nose shape, distance between eyes, size of the mouth and chin or—what was most noticeable—the shade and texture of the hair. The rose-pearly skin always stayed immaculate, also their bodies were nearly identical, with a narrow waist, large busts, and quite wide in the hips, in line with the currently prevailing standard of beauty. Raina was rather small, had light chocolate-colored skin, curly black hair, and huge, very dark eyes, oblong like leaves. It was immediately apparent that her appearance was individually programmed, and didn't come from the ready template. Guillermo Hernan, lost without a trace, had to have approached his order with great engagement, so it was even sadder to see extensive traces of deliberate damage on the synthetic body.

"Someone tortured her," Etta whispered in horror. Something like that was incomprehensible for her, though she wasn't sure if androids felt pain in any form. The *Andropology* textbook claimed they were aware of the damage and that it was uncomfortable for them. What exactly that discomfort was, the manual did not specify.

"Many people wouldn't put it this way." Dr. O'Leary crouched down by the bed and began to diagnose Raina methodically. "For them, an android is just a mannequin, and what could be wrong with hitting a dummy with a bat?"

He took out a tool from his briefcase and looked with it into Raina's eyes. Then he shook his head in disgust, changed the scanner to another one and took the blanket off Raina, revealing her beautifully modeled body, long legs, gorgeous waist and tiny, sharp-ended breasts. She resembled drawings from the Egyptian tombs. The prone android allowed the cyberneticians to study her with such indifference, as if she were indeed just an object.

"Is she like this all the time?" Etta asked Raul, who was standing beside her.

"No," he replied. "Only since yesterday morning. Before that, we could make a contact with her. Brent thinks she has damaged synapses."

"He is right," Leonard said, who was writing down what his boss was dictating in a low voice, without interrupting the exam. "I hoped we could help her here on the spot, but unfortunately, it's not possible. We have to take her to the center. We are dealing not only with mechanical damage to the outer shell and broken ribs, but also a severe degeneration of the synaptic filler, and a lot of internal injuries, including a torn, ehm, sexual feature."

"Name the things by their names, don't play the antique monk," O'Leary snarled. "There is a woman with us, but I would bet that she wasn't born yesterday, and the word 'vagina' isn't new to her. No offense, Miss Solis, but this brother-in-law of yours is a dangerous nutcase! I don't know what tool he used to do this to her, but it must have been something sizeable. Maybe a baseball bat or something like that. Where did your sister find that guy? She is lucky she's still alive, with such a husband... and such a bastard had been bringing up two children! The social guardian of his neighborhood should hang himself immediately."

The doctor was obviously agitated, though he tried to hide it. There was no trace left of his usual stoicism and indifference. Social guardians were part of the so-called public trust department. People usually believed that the curators saw everything and knew everything. They trusted their judgment, and consulted them when in difficult situations. The thought that one of them had neglected his duties to such an extent was extremely unpleasant.

"Will you help her?" Raul asked. His voice was as pure and calm as ever. It merely conveyed the intention of acquiring the information, but the people present in the room seemed to hear also the tone of anxiety in it.

"Certainly, but not here. We have to take her to the research center. It will be a job for at least six hours, and not just for the two of us. Leo, call the technicians and tell them to prepare the room and the tool set for a full general operation, and let them order a new chemogel from formula C-8 from Dr. Ponce. Let them also announce the high alert for the plastic technicians— there will be a lot of reconstruction here."

"Will you exchange her brain?" Etta asked with a slight tremor. The thought itself seemed absurd, but she understood that it worked that way.

"What an idea!" O'Leary snorted contemptuously. "Women. A brain can't be exchanged, my dear lady, it's a rigid grid of microcircuits. But it is possible to exchange the chemogel that, by mechanical interaction, has begun to produce defective synapses. Anyway, it's way over your head. We are taking this girl."

"Can she walk on her own?"

"We'll see. Leo, give her a stir."

The assistant pulled out a small object from his briefcase and touched the middle of Raina's chest with it. There was a light crackle, a blue spark leaped, and then the naked, damaged body twitched. The black deer-like eyes grew brighter and slowly looked around. Then a raspy, stuttering voice said, "Who... is... here?"

"I'm a cybernetician. I'll fix your body. Can you get up and walk with me to the research center?"

"I don't know... if it is possible. My Dominant... may... not... agree."

O'Leary sighed and ran his hand through his graying hair.

"Raina, who is your Dominant?" he asked.

"Licenziato Da... rio Cantoralle."

"No, Raina. He isn't your Dominant," the doctor said emphatically.

"No...?"

"No. Your Dominant is Guillermo Hernan, lost without a trace. Probably dead, otherwise he would have been found long ago. Dario Cantoralle stole you, appropriated you, and has no rights to you."

Raina moved her beautifully outlined lips as if trying to find some matching words. She let out a rattling sound several times, like a dying old-fashioned clock with a pendulum.

"He's dead," she finally said mechanically. "Not... alive. So who will be... taking care of me?"

O'Leary and his assistant exchanged glances. Etta bit her lips nervously.

"Me," Leonard said finally. "From now on, I am your Dominant. Repeat: My Dominant is Leonard Derkacz."

"My… Do… m… in… ant… is Leo… nnnnard… Derrrrr…"

"That's fine," O'Leary cut in. "Don't exert yourself, Raina, you have a broken speech apparatus. Raul, could you carry her? Better not let her walk on her own. Her soul is hardly sticking to her. Electric soul, of course," he added hurriedly.

Raul wrapped Raina in a blanket and took her in his arms. She allowed for it passively, her curly head falling on his arm like a sick child's. She was so helpless at that moment that the girl watching her felt her throat close and hated her brother-in-law more than ever.

"Where should I take her, Doctor?" Raul asked.

"To the control center. The science department."

*****

The recovery operation, as Leonard described repairing the damaged android, had been underway for several hours. Etta couldn't explain why she didn't want to go to her quarters. It was strange, but sitting in the corridor of the scientific department, she felt as if she was sitting at the door of the room in which a member of her family was being operated on. It was a bit absurd, since she had only met Raina today, but the dark-skinned android seemed to her so weak, helpless, and somehow humanly frail, that despite all logic she felt responsible for her. Maybe part of the reason was that it was her brother-in-law who put this innocent, pure creature in such a miserable state?

"And to think I was once in love with Dario…" she muttered at last with a shudder of disgust. She couldn't understand now what she had once seen in him. True, he was very handsome, but how did it happen that she hadn't noticed his arrogance earlier, the drive to dominate his environment, and his sadistic aspirations?

The Companion sitting beside her looked at her, his head slightly inclined. In the gestures of the beings similar to him, this meant a silent question which they could not express with their imperfect mimicry.

"Never mind," she answered, though he didn't ask the question aloud. "Tell me something. Why was it you who told us about her? Why not Rasmus? Doesn't he trust his Domina?"

Raul smiled suddenly, in an android way, awkwardly and artificially, but with unexpected spontaneity.

"But he did tell her," he said. "Brent trusts Miss Hornet and has no secrets from her."

"So why didn't she…?"

"Miss Hornet couldn't officially do anything. It's strictly confidential so far, but she's CCM. She could not."

"What?!"

"Rather, who. Coordinator of Civilian Migration. It's a latent function for now. Even though she has passed the officers' test, Miss Hornet will not be on the military list, for the general good. She asked me to go with this issue to Dr. O'Leary."

Etta put a hand on his shoulder and shook her head slightly.

"Raul, what would I do without you? You always know everything. What do you think, will Raina recover?"

"I don't have detailed data to evaluate. But we all want that. Estrella, why didn't Dr. O'Leary become the new Dominant of Raina?"

"Because he doesn't want to have obligations. Leonard is more organized, I would say, more thoughtful, more responsible. And I think this poor thing will require special care."

Contrary to common sense, she thought of Raina as a human. She couldn't think otherwise. Whenever she tried to make herself realize that it was just a combination of microcircuits and functional processors, the memory of the flowers next to the android's mattress appeared before her eyes. True, living flowers, put into a tin cup with water. An element unusual in its simplicity and logically unnecessary.

"Raul, do you copy the behavior of people or are you at least a little spontaneous?" she asked seriously. "I have to know."

"And what is spontaneity?" the Companion answered with a question. "Does it exist? You surely don't know the textbook of human behaviorism, written by an android named Rivas 34A. He wrote, "A human appears in the world in a larval stage, with a completely blank mind. During maturation, it changes his physical proportions and acquires experience. He processes the collected information into schemes, ready-to-use, depending on the circumstances." This is a very important observation, Etta. It means that something like spontaneity is much less tangible than it is generally thought. People apply to new situations the experiences they have acquired in the past and remembered consciously or unconsciously. We... we do the same."

"Rasmus brought Raina flowers. Why?"

"So that she would have a sign that we think of her, even when we are not with her. Don't people give flowers for the same reason?"

It was difficult to deny sense to this reasoning. Anyway, androids were always precisely logical, it couldn't be any other way. At the higher stage of computer development, they took over their model of thought operations, and modern technology only allowed them to refine it.

"You know, I still know so little about you," Etta whispered softly, leaning her head on Raul's shoulder, but soon she jumped with fear.

The door of the studio opened with a bang, and Dr. O'Leary walked out into the corridor. He held a cap in his hand that he had just taken off his head, and ruffled his already untidy hair with his other hand.

"Oh, you still here?" he asked politely. "Did something happen?"

"No. I wanted to know if everything went well," the girl explained, jumping from her chair, which immediately folded and slid into the wall.

"Why should anything go wrong? Yes, the procedure was tedious, but it was not the first time I repaired a damaged android. Although I must admit, that it was first one damaged in this way. We need another week for stabilization and the girl will be able to start to learn how to live."

Etta smiled with involuntary gratitude. The doctor returned her smile. Although he didn't talk about it, he was glad someone else shared his love and respect for the androids. It was a rare and precious phenomenon.

"Since you are here already, you should report to Gongadze," he said after a moment, remembering something. "He has something important to tell you. And I want to see you tomorrow at eight in my workshop for the exam. Based on the results, I will decide if you are material for a future android specialist."

"Of course, Doctor."

Leonard escorted Raina, dressed only in a short shirt, into the corridor. She looked much better already, although she was still walking awkwardly. It was clear that her sense of balance had not returned to normal yet, but her chocolate skin had been repaired so perfectly that it was impossible to tell where it had been removed from the artificial muscles, and the polymeric eyes had gained some expression. She was immaculately beautiful, though at the same time completely different from the types of female androids well known to Etta. All distortions had been perfectly removed, as if they never existed. The plastic technicians did a good job, and it could be expected that Dr. O'Leary and his assistant did equally well repairing the internal damage. Etta regretted not being able to stay, but she had to run to the coordinator's office. Since the lieutenant colonel wanted to talk to her, the matter had to be important. Raina's rehabilitation would be dealt with by O'Leary and Derkacz, her new Dominant. They would surely supervise it better than Etta. She was redundant here.

However, as she walked out, she caught a glimpse of the android, and, contrary to all logic, she could swear she could see a sign of sympathy. Then Raina smiled awkwardly and raised her hand in a farewell gesture.

XIII

We have to do it," Tengiz Gongadze said emphatically. For him, too, this matter was difficult. He was a father himself, and besides, he didn't have a heart of stone. However, the most important people at the center had decided at the meeting that this would be the best solution. Itati and Amador were supposed to be taken by a foster family. Their father was locked up in prison, which he probably wouldn't leave for the rest of his life, even if he somehow escaped execution. And her mother was in a psychiatric clinic and it wasn't sure how she would be qualified. As the jointly composed opinion for the family court said, it would be better for the children to be with people who are a model family. Dr. Gongadze stroked his mustache nervously. He would rather not make such a decision, but since the whole story happened in his jurisdiction, he had to face it.

"Unfortunately we have to do that." Etta was clearly depressed, but didn't protest. "But I don't understand why Raul should go with them, and not me? These children have some prejudices against artificial life forms. I feel they are afraid of them."

"Especially because of that. Traveling under the care of an android can teach them more than any lecture. Anyway, we have this order that once you come to the resort, no man can leave it. Except pilots. These little kids are an exception, because they do not know what's going on anyway, and Raul is not human. Do you understand?"

Etta suppressed a desire to scratch her head. This whole story with the various precautions seemed to her very stupid, but she still felt relieved with the decision to put her niece and nephew up for adoption. After all, the family court could have demanded that she take care of them, and she didn't feel like it. She couldn't imagine working with her sister's children. They were both afraid of her after the incident during the briefing and didn't trust her a bit. It was especially sad because Etta generally got along well with kids, and loved them so much. Otherwise, she wouldn't have chosen to work as a primary school teacher.

"And if they won't want to listen to him?" she asked.

"You have to convince them. Surely the prospect of driving to their grandparents will be, for them, reassuring. Until the family court makes a final decision, they will need to stay there. I hope your parents are okay?"

Etta shrugged. What could she answer? That they were very okay, just not toward her? The colonel didn't care about her experiences, since they concerned only her. In the end, Amador and his sister were twos, so they had the opportunities that fate had denied her. Their grandparents would surely treat them well.

"They can stay there," she said finally. "At least until the court assigns a foster family. Poor kids, but I can't help them. They have bad luck to have such parents. The grandparents certainly love them and are proud of them. They weren't so kind with me."

"What can you do? It happens. It is good that you take it calmly."

"I am not going to get hysterical like Nayeli. It wouldn't help anything anyway. I guess I even feel relieved not to have to deal with my family. This whole situation is very awkward for me, and besides, my work excludes raising children at the moment."

That meeting was not the only unpleasant part of her day. What happened later was also not a pleasure. She had to explain to the pair of frightened kids that they would travel to their grandparents without their mom or dad, but instead would be under the care of an android. It was clear that both of them were raised with a real phobia of androids—Amador dared to kick Raul only because he had his mother nearby. In a different situation, he would just run away from him. The thought that he was going to be alone with an android made him even bluer from crying than Itati, who, as the younger sibling, understood less of what was going on but joined her brother's sobbing in solidarity. Etta had to be patient and reassure both her niece and nephew for quite some time.

"Raul will not do anything to you. He will protect you and if you wish, he won't say a word the whole way," she explained. "Androids aren't dangerous at all, they help people. They do no harm to anyone."

But it didn't bring the required effect. The children were really scared, too scared to accept logical arguments. Even though they had been avoiding their aunt before, they clung to her desperately now and kept repeating between their sobs that they wouldn't go anywhere. Finally, they calmed a bit after the promise that they would be able to visit their mom in Montepietro after her discharge from the hospital, while it wouldn't be possible if they stayed at the center. But even then, the children didn't give up easily.

"But Auntie, you take us there, okay? Please, please…"

"We will be nice, we promise, we will be quiet the whole way."

Etta's heart melted under the touch of the small hands, and she almost began to cry, too. It did no good that she repeatedly told herself she was a tough lieutenant in the service of the global government, she couldn't manage to keep her tone of voice dry. She would have probably given in if not for Veronica, who fortunately appeared in the quarters. She understood the situation from the first sight and immediately took over the charges.

"Enough of this, kids," she said in the firm voice. "Estrella Solis, shame on you! Since when were you are not able to handle a couple of toddlers? In addition, you should explain yourself to such kids as before your own commander. Listen, striplings—you are going to your grandparents under Raul's care. This is an official command and you have no say in this. Now, calm down!"

The children went silent, only whimpering quietly, and looked at Veronica with respect.

"That's how it is done. Now wipe their noses and pack their stuff instead of making a sad dogface. The speed car is already waiting, and the pilot and Raul are with the old man. Hurry up, girl! I will help you, it will be faster."

Etta nodded obediently. Veronica has always been a voice of reason in their small group. Disciplined, logical, and strong, she decided everything, and Etta surrendered to her even when she wasn't sure about her arguments. Since they'd gotten to know each other, Veronica had been the boss, and Etta agreed to all her ideas. And not only her. The daughter of Rosalie and Gerry Hornet had always influenced people around her. She got it from her father, an overbearing and violent man. She had the ability to impose her will on others, and people listened to her without objections. She would be a great military woman if she chose to remain on this path.

*****

While the two girls were in the Cantoralle quarters, Raul and the young pilot of the Eurasian unit received the latest guidelines from the coordinator's office, now occupied by Tengiz Gongadze.

"Immediately after arriving in Montepietro, you will fill up on fuel and deliver the package with documents to the local management unit," the lieutenant colonel said to the pilot, who was standing at attention in front of him.

He then handed the quiet android the encoded type-B pod used for transferring official documentation.

"When you leave the children in their place, you will bring this to the family court in Montepietro, Bolivar Street, Number Five. Unfortunately, in these cases medieval procedures still apply, and court documents must be delivered personally. You will receive a confirmation of receipt."

"Yes, Colonel," Raul replied shortly. He took the pod and placed it carefully in his uniform pocket. Even if he had an opinion about the whole thing, he didn't show a sign of it.

Tengiz Gongadze looked at him carefully and added, "I know you're the best when it comes to caring for kids. Timmy loves you since the time you saved him from the pool, and the rest of the children treat you like a human, but these two are different. You know that, right?"

"Yes I know. They were raised hating artificial intelligence."

"You don't mind?"

"Their attitude toward me is irrelevant. I have to deliver them so I will do it."

"Wait. And you? Will you be able to be neutral toward them?"

Lieutenant Colonel Gongadze didn't know where that question had come from. Before he came to this center, he didn't care about androids and their inner life. In fact, he didn't even believe that artificials had any independent personality. They were scarce in the army, and in any case they were an exception. Some of the officers had Companions, but not all units tolerated that. Gongadze had had virtually no contact with the androids, even with MA, the medical androids that worked in some hospitals as nurses and technicians. It was only when he found himself in this center that he met a few of them and realized that they were not robots but living forms, though devoid of two basic aspects of the popular definition of life—metabolism, and the possibility of self-replication. But he still didn't know how to treat them.

"I will not hurt the protohumans," Raul said gently.

"I know. Of course you won't. But do you... do you feel bad? I mean, discomfort because of the behavior of these kids?"

Raul inclined his head slightly.

"Only if they could threaten me themselves," he replied. "Words can't damage."

Gongadze suddenly became convinced that android wasn't telling him the truth, or in any case, not the whole truth. His face had to be easy to decipher, as Raul suddenly added:

"Please understand, Colonel, the names that define what we feel have not been created yet. It's like the difference between electric potentials, varying, depending on the situation. Nobody has given them detailed names yet."

"Does that mean you really feel?" Gongadze stammered with the horror he couldn't hide. What he really feared as a doctor had really happened—the pride of the researchers had caused a new type of man to be created. Artificial from head to toe, but just as human as himself. And his innate sense of justice required him to admit that he had the same rights to a place under the sun as his creators.

Raul looked at him with that gentle calmness, as if he understood well what shocked the man in front of him.

"Yes," he answered simply. "We feel. Not quite like you, built from protein molecules and controlled by chromosomes, but we feel. You are affected by hormones and gland enzymes, and we by the differences in potentials in circuits. That's why it is difficult to use the same terms to describe them, and new ones don't exist yet."

A compelling logic. It would be difficult indeed. The lieutenant colonel stroked his mustache nervously, then shrugged.

"Please go," he finally said officially, and started to look through the documents, trying to look much more occupied than he was.

*****

At the same time, Veronica and Etta finished packing the Cantoralles' stuff. Apart from the missing migration plan, they also found a lot of coded notes and various objects whose use wasn't easy to guess—they put them aside to pass to the colonel. Fortunately, everything pointed to the fact that Dario had no collaborators at the center.

"Of course, we can't be completely sure," Veronica said. "But it seems to me that he was acting in this alone. I hope it was really so."

"If not, the investigation will reveal his partners," Etta murmured. She felt dejected and tired, as if she hadn't slept for a week.

Veronica shook her head slowly.

"There is no time for that. Our time is coming soon. Very soon..."

"Seriously?! When?!"

"Shhh. I only know it will be soon. The order will probably arrive within the next thirty-six hours."

Etta sat on the nearest chair, as if she suddenly lost her strength. Now that the departure was inevitable, when it was no longer possible to withdraw, a sudden anxiety overwhelmed her, so strong she began to tremble. Her friend wrapped her arm around her.

"Hold on," she whispered. "We have to be strong. And we will not be alone. Understand? We will never be alone anymore."

*****

The triangular airplane flew through the clouds. The android was sitting in the back seat, with the silent, sulking children on both sides. The pilot paid no attention to them and hummed cheerfully at the controls, careful not to go off course. The vehicle was not too fast, just like all the mini-planes, so the flight would take several hours, which for the two children was stretching indefinitely. If their guardian had been a man, they would probably talk him to death, but raised in distrust of the androids, they didn't want to speak to Raul. They partly ignored his presence, partly were afraid of him... either way, they stayed silent. Raul didn't speak either, so that there was silence in the soundproof passenger cabin, interrupted only by the gentle noise of the microenvironment control apparatus and the whistling of the pilot, as the cabin and cockpit were connected. The young boy in uniform didn't probably like silence. He was alternately humming and whistling popular hits, and he apparently knew them all. He didn't repeat the same melody twice. Raul listened to him, trying to catch some mathematical sense in the lyrics. He never understood the nature of singing or why it was so valuable to people. Melodies were only empty sounds for him, no different from those of the working engine.

The pilot was human and therefore he could love music. At some point, however, he stopped in the middle of the song "Midnight in the City" and cleared his throat somehow strangely.

"Attention..." he began, and at the same time the vehicle began to thrash around in the air.

"What's going on?!" Amador shouted, grabbing the arm of the chair. Itati howled with fear and her face grew pale.

"Turbulence," Raul said, and paused as the plane shook again.

"We flew into an unannounced storm front!" the pilot shouted. "Hold on, it's going to be a rough ride!"

The children shouted in unison and clung to Raul, grabbing his arms. Suddenly their reluctance turned into a boundless trust in someone who was their guarantee of security, as promised by a little-known aunt.

"Calm down." He reached, not without some effort, for the emergency button. After he pressed the red button, a kind of cocoon was closed around the three passengers, like a huge flower—a spore. Although sea creatures wouldn't threaten castaways in the long-dead oceans, a fall into rough water would end badly if not for this practical invention. It had a supply of water and vitaminized nutritional pellets, and the wall-mounted sensors monitored the carbon dioxide content, turning on the purifying circulation and adding oxygen from high-pressure tanks if necessary. The structure of the spore allowed for survival until rescue, even if it took several days.

The plane was still staggering and shivering like a drunk, and though the sound of the storm didn't reach the cockpit, they felt that the storm had to be really powerful.

"Calm down," Raul repeated. "This life-saving cocoon is practically indestructible. Even if a catastrophe happens, nothing will happen to us, and emergency services will find us."

His words didn't seem to calm the frightened children. Each time the plane jerked, they squealed with fear, hugging under his shoulders. Although they had previously avoided the android, they now clung to him from both sides with such absolute trust, as if their father had never ingrained them with a fear of such beings. Raul embraced caringly both little trembling bodies. He knew from his own observation that the toddlers needed it, and even though it was an illogical need, it did exist and he had to take care of it. It was his assignment, entrusted by his Domina, and no android would disregard such orders.

The little plane was flying ahead in the furious gusts of the stormy wind, struggling with the force of nature that was pushing it off course. It lasted for exactly thirteen and half minutes. Then the flight suddenly leveled off, and after a moment, the vehicle floated softly on the landing strip and stopped.

"All right now, you can open the cocoon," the cheerful voice of the pilot could be heard in the relay. "Abe Holmes made a miracle once again."

It took a few more minutes before Raul managed to persuade the scared children that they were safe now. The kids were clearly shaken and didn't want to let go of him, but the patience and calmness of the android finally had its effect. The children stopped crying, allowed him to open the spore, and got off the plane onto the landing strip where a military limousine with a social curator and a properly trained babysitter were waiting for them.

"Hey, artificial!" the pilot called. "I'll get the fuel and deliver that stuff they told me, but it won't take long. Be here before two, okay?"

"I will," Raul answered laconically. He helped the children to get into the vehicle and sat down next to them. The behavior of the pilot Holmes was something common—people generally treated the androids like that, but the word used by the young soldier caused a discomfort in his perception circuits. If Raul was a man, he might say he simply didn't like the pilot. But it wasn't the time to think about it now. Another confrontation with Etta's parents was waiting for him, and it might be difficult. He had never seen them before and didn't know what they were like. After all, they could share Dario's opinions.

But it wasn't that bad. Miranda and Jair Solis didn't pay any attention to him at all, and they took care of the curator and the babysitter, preparing them a quick snack. They already knew about their daughter's illness and that their son-in-law had been arrested for murder, so seeing their grandchildren was a big surprise to them. Watching the elders hug and kiss the children, as they clung to them with confidence and relief, Raul discovered something with all the amazement an android could be capable of. He realized that he couldn't tell them what the family court would probably decide. He didn't understand why something kept him from revealing the truth, but this something existed somewhere deep within his circuits. Was his silence of any importance against the facts, though?

After leaving unnoticed and shutting the door behind him, he went to the local office of the family court. He didn't have to take a speed car. Like all the androids, he marched confidently and quickly, and the building wasn't far from the Solises' apartment. However, in the middle of his journey, he stopped and took the encoded pod out of the inner pocket of his uniform. He had time. He had almost an hour until it was time to meet the pilot who would take him back to the center. He carefully touched the sensors of the flat device. He knew military coding systems good enough to be able to break each of them, and this one didn't look complicated. He moved his fingers over the sensors quickly, almost imperceptibly, until he finally found the right key. He skimmed the case description and focused on the final conclusion:

In view of the above, it is advisable to remove the parental rights of the Solis-Cantoralle pair and to transfer the two minors, Itati and Amador Cantoralle, to one of the selected foster families. Care must be taken to ensure that their biological parents don't have any contact with them in the future.

The android froze for a moment. He returned in his thoughts to the image of Mr. and Ms. Solis holding their grandchildren, then the image of hysterical Nayeli appeared, followed by a picture of Itati and Amador, holding his arms convulsively during the turbulence. Protohuman... special protection. What did Estrella say when she was seeing them to the speed car?

"Remember, take care of them. Their good is most important. Promise me that you will take care of this."

He promised, of course. Only what was the real good of the child? How to predict what could really harm them? *The Rivas Handbook*, the only book written by an android for androids, defined child-family relations as a reflection of the Companion-Dominant relationship. If that was the case—Raul couldn't know whether it was really true—severing of this bond had to cause fatal psychological trauma to the immature individual. Its development could be disturbed irreversibly.

Raul moved his fingers over the sensors again. Slowly, a letter at the time, he changed the text:

In view of the above, it is advisable to remove the parental rights of the Solis-Cantoralle pair and to transfer the two minors, Itati and Amador Cantoralle, to the care of the parents of their biological mother. Nayeli Solis de Cantoralle can see them after completing her treatment, in the presence of their legal guardians.

He put back the encoding, carefully erasing all traces of his manipulation. He closed the pod and put it back in his pocket. For a moment he stood there, staring into space as he always did while analyzing a problem. A passing police motorcycle slowed down, but the policeman driving it accelerated again, seeing a metal triangle in his earlobe. An artificial didn't constitute a public danger like someone emotionally disturbed enough to roam aimlessly in the street. Raul didn't even notice him.

"Protohuman... special protection," he finally said quietly before continuing on his way.

He was alone on the sidewalk. People were driving up to it just to get off and go where they were going. Freaks going to walk on foot to the store were rare. Even if someone heard Raul's whisper, they wouldn't understand who he was talking to and why. If they would even pay attention at all to the words of an android... an artificial form of existence.

THE END

Please read *The Convoy*, Part II of *The Legend of the Future* series.